PURRFECT HEIST

THE MYSTERIES OF MAX 89

NIC SAINT

PURRFECT HEIST

The Mysteries of Max 89

Copyright © 2024 by Nic Saint

All rights reserved. No part of this book may be reproduced in any form by any electronic or mechanical means including photocopying, recording, or information storage and retrieval without permission in writing from the author.

This is a work of fiction. Names, characters, places, brands, media, and incidents are either the product of the author's imagination or are used fictitiously. The author acknowledges the trademarked status and trademark owners of various products referenced in this work of fiction, which have been used without permission. The publication/use of these trademarks is not authorized, associated with, or sponsored by the trademark owners.

Edited by Chereese Graves

www.nicsaint.com

Give feedback on the book at: info@nicsaint.com

facebook.com/nicsaintauthor
@nicsaintauthor

First Edition

Printed in the U.S.A

PURRFECT HEIST

The Gray Panthers Ride Again

You know that when a shot rings out in the early morning, it can't be good. And so when we arrived at the scene and found our neighbor Kurt Mayfield bleeding on the ground, it gave us quite a shock. At the same time, across town, a museum was being burgled by a gang of dedicated gangsters. Were the two events connected? It was up to us to find out. In the meantime we also had to deal with Gran having developed a habit of sleepwalking, a distressed Papillon dog, a dog whisperer with a secret agenda and a collection of Nazi art. In other words: business as usual!

CHAPTER 1

Dooley had been keeping a close eye on his human for the last couple of days, and when he saw her traipsing through Blake's Field in her underwear, he knew that his concerns had been justified all along. Even his best friend Max had told him that he was exaggerating and that Gran was fine. Obviously she wasn't fine. She was anything but fine. But since Max was home, he couldn't tell him that he had been right and that Max was wrong. Not that he would have done so, since that wasn't Dooley's style.

He followed Gran from a little distance, making sure she didn't notice she was being followed. She wouldn't have liked it since she was a proud old lady and wouldn't have condoned a chaperone in the form of her own kitty. He wondered where she was going and why she would venture out of the house in the middle of the night, only dressed in her undies. The situation was certainly cause for grave concern. He followed her all the way to the small derelict shack that was still located on the field and hadn't been taken down, even though the entire neighborhood had asked the field's owner many times.

He watched from a safe distance as Gran took a seat in front of the shack, on a crooked bench that had seen better days, and folded her hands in her lap, sitting prim and proper. Then she reached into her pocket and took out a bag containing something he couldn't quite make out. She reached into the bag, and the next moment started singing softly to herself. *"Feed the birds,"* she sang. *"Feed the birds. Tuppence a bag. Tuppence a bag."* And as he watched on in amazement and a rising sense of concern, she started strewing breadcrumbs from the bag. But since it was the middle of the night, there weren't any birds present to partake in this moderate feast. Instead, a couple of the mice that lived in the old shack emerged from their hiding places, sniffed the air for a moment, and then descended on the breadcrumbs, gobbling them up with relish.

So now Gran had taken to feeding the mice? But why? He simply didn't understand what was going on, except that he should probably tell somebody before one of the neighbors noticed Gran's strange behavior and had her locked up in an institution.

He wondered for a moment if he shouldn't approach the old lady and tell her to go back to bed. He had been lying at the foot of her bed when she had ventured out, but when he had asked her where she thought she was going, she hadn't replied, but had simply slipped her feet into her slippers and had left the house. And since he didn't want her to get into trouble, he had decided to follow her and see where she was going.

As he watched, she crumpled up the bag and put it back into her pocket, then rocked back and forth for a moment, humming the same tune under her breath, a happy smile on her face. She was staring before her, seemingly looking at nothing in particular.

The mice had dispensed with the last pieces of bread and

returned to their nest to deliver the good news that a new benefactor was in town and that they might be looking forward to many more nights like this, with Gran delivering food to their little home.

Dooley knew the mice since he had made their acquaintance on several occasions, and he could only applaud their good fortune. It still didn't allay his general sense of unease at this type of behavior from one who he had always admired and loved.

He now wondered if he should tell Marge that her mother had developed this strange new habit of feeding the mice. Marge would worry, of course, since she was that kind of person. But that couldn't be helped. At least she would tell Tex, and the doctor could take a closer look at the strange behavior his mother-in-law had started displaying lately.

For this wasn't the first time Gran had ventured out like this, though mostly she had limited her nocturnal sojourn to the backyard. This was the first time she had ventured out beyond the perimeter of her own home. If this kept up, pretty soon she would start wandering all over Hampton Cove, or even the entire island or maybe the state.

As he watched on, he saw that a dark figure had appeared, hiding behind a nearby tree. The dark figure was watching Gran, biding his time. Dooley's heart jumped into his throat when he realized that his human might be in some kind of grave danger.

Gran hadn't noticed the dark figure, but then she wasn't in a state to notice much of anything right now. He wondered if he should warn her that she was being watched.

Then again, it might be one of the neighbors walking their dog in the middle of the night and wondering what Gran was up to. They could be excused for wanting to know what was going on—the same way Dooley wanted to know what she was up to.

He saw that the figure detached themselves from that tree and approached Gran. He still couldn't make out their face or other distinguishing features, but it was clear that the figure was just as curious to find out what was going on as he himself was.

The figure walked right up to Gran and stood before her. Gran still didn't react in any meaningful way, and that's when Dooley understood: she was sleepwalking!

He had heard about this kind of behavior, where people get out of bed in the middle of the night and do all kinds of stuff that they later don't remember. It was not a good thing, especially since she was away from home and vulnerable, as the situation showed.

His words of warning were stuck in his throat, or he would have called out to Gran to wake up and get out of there. For the person had taken out what looked like a great big knife and now stood wielding it in front of Gran's face. The old lady was still smiling and didn't seem to notice what was going on.

The figure must have realized that she formed no threat whatsoever, for he or she put the knife away again, waved a hand in front of Gran's eyes, then shrugged and took off.

Dooley breathed a sigh of relief, and even more so when Gran finally got up and started on the short trek home.

It wasn't long before she was crawling back into bed and dragging the covers over her ears. Dooley eyed her for a few moments from his vantage point at the foot of the bed. But when he heard his human's slow and even breathing, he finally lay down his head and slept.

Tomorrow he would tell Marge. Clearly, something had to be done.

CHAPTER 2

Kurt Mayfield was walking his dog Fifi and wondering not for the first time if his time couldn't be better spent some other, more productive, way. After all, Fifi had the use of the entire backyard, and if she wanted to, even the field behind the house, though he normally didn't condone that she snuck underneath the fence.

Still, dogs needed to be walked, or so common sense dictated. And it was true that there was an added benefit in that he got to satisfy one of his secret pastimes: spying on his neighbors. Nobody appreciated it when you blatantly took up position in front of their homes and stared into their living rooms and watched what they did. But when you held a dog on the leash, it was accepted behavior. What he didn't like about dog walking was that you ran the risk of bumping into other dog walkers, and invariably they would engage him in conversation, asking questions about this or that, generally making a nuisance of themselves. This is why he had adopted the practice of walking Fifi very early in the morning, at six o'clock, and late at night, just before he went to bed. That way, the risk of running into his neighboring blabbermouths was a lot less. Some of them had even started a WhatsApp group and arranged to walk their dogs together. To Kurt, that was what hell must be like. He had kindly declined to be added to the group.

Gilda, his neighbor and also his girlfriend, often told him he was a curmudgeon, and she probably had a point. But then after sixty-eight years of being a grouch, what were the chances that he would ever change? Once a grouch, always a grouch, and he riposted by telling her that she seemed to like him anyway, to which she admitted this was true.

"I have tamed the grouch of Harrington Street," she said laughingly. "And I should probably deserve some kind of prize."

Funny girl.

He passed by Blake's Field and Fifi, as was her habit, yanked and strained at the leash to take a peek inside their local jungle. Years of neglect had turned the field into a haven of weeds and trees and shrubs, and if he had complained to the town council once, he had complained a million times. Ownership of the field was in some kind of legal limbo at the moment, and as long as the lawyers representing the previous owners and the town council didn't get their act together and turn it into something that was a boon to the neighborhood instead of an eyesore, there was nothing anyone could do about it.

At least it wasn't a big building pit, for once upon a time there had been plans to develop the land, which would have been imminently worse if it had gone through.

"All right, all right," he said as Fifi barked up a storm. "I'll bite." Probably she wanted to take a look at that old shack, which seemed to hold a special appeal to the little Yorkie. Once upon a time she had even found a dead body there. It had been quite the scandal. A murder, in a pleasant neighborhood like theirs? Absolutely unheard of.

He hurried after Fifi, hoping he didn't step into something nasty. Since he wasn't the only dog owner who used Blake's Field to allow their beloved mutts some off-leash time, the grass had been trampled on and flattened and a natural sort of pathway had formed that led from the street to the shack. He could have followed it with his eyes closed since he had walked this same route many times with Fifi.

She barked happily when they finally reached the old shack, and the moment he unleashed her, she started prancing around and happily jumping up against his legs.

He smiled and affectionately patted her on the head.

"Go on, girl," he said encouragingly. "You go on."

This was her time, and she knew it.

He took a seat on the bench that had been placed in front of the shack and watched as his little doggie disappeared into the high weeds that surrounded the shack. From time to time he saw her jumping up, her head briefly clearing the weeds and shrubs, then she was gone again, possibly chasing a rabbit or some other creature of the undergrowth.

The shack itself was home to a colony of mice, and he suspected there were also plenty of rats and other vermin housed there. From time to time a chicken would pop its head up. They used to belong to Ted Trapper but had escaped captivity and were now roaming wild and free, just like all the other creatures that occupied this plot of land.

He didn't mind, as long as they didn't cross the boundary with his backyard and enter his private property. Even the vermin of this world should know its place.

He glanced around, and when he didn't see anyone, took a small silver case out of his jacket pocket, extracted a cigarette, and lit one up. As he took a long drag, he closed his eyes with relish and directed a plume of smoke at the sky.

Gilda had told him that smoking was a filthy habit, and to accommodate her, he had cut down to two ciggies a day: one during each time he took Fifi for her walks. Another benefit of having a dog.

As he fixed his eyes on a point in the distance where he knew his house was located, he thought he saw something bright red hanging from a nearby tree. He frowned as he got up. As far as he could tell, he had never seen anything hanging from that tree before. Maybe another dog walker had accidentally left it behind? Or maybe kids had been playing there, even though most of the parents living on this block strictly forbade their offspring from venturing out there, since there were rumors that drug addicts used the shack to engage in their favorite pastime. In other words: not exactly a playground.

He walked up to the tree and saw that the red item was a sweater. He took it down and studied it. No name tag. It looked new and probably belonged to someone who was missing it now. He wondered if he should take it along to give to his neighbor Chase Kingsley. The cop could take it into the station with him and drop it off at the lost-and-found. As he folded up the sweater, something fell out of a hidden pocket. It was a piece of jewelry, and as he picked it up from the ground, he saw that it was a little golden cross. Very nice, he thought as he turned it over in his hand. And probably expensive. There were markings on the cross, but since he hadn't taken his reading glasses along with him, he couldn't quite make them out. He closed his fist around the little trinket and was more determined now to hand it over to Chase. He'd know what to do with it.

He returned to the bench to finish his smoke when he thought he saw movement in the shrubbery nearby. "Fifi?" he said. But it wasn't Fifi who emerged. It was a large person wearing a hoodie, which partially obscured his or her face.

Before he could ask what they were doing there, the stranger took out a gun and pulled the trigger. Kurt felt a stinging pain in his chest, and as he went down, he thought that of all the things that could happen to a person walking his dog, the oddest had to be to get shot and killed.

Poor Fifi. Now what would become of her?

CHAPTER 3

I had been idly glancing out of the upstairs bedroom window when I thought I heard a loud bang. The kind of bang that only a gun can make. As it seemed to be coming from Blake's Field, I wondered if perhaps someone had taken advantage of the early hour to go and do some hunting. As everyone knows, there are plenty of rabbits that have made the field their home, and some people seem to enjoy rabbit meat as much as others like chicken or beef.

Next to me, my friend Dooley also looked up. "What was that?" he asked.

"Sounded like a gunshot," I said. "Coming from Blake's Field."

He shook his head. "I'm telling you, Max, ever since Gran started walking around in the middle of the night, I haven't slept a wink."

I could have told him this was a blatant lie, for I had seen him—and heard him—sleep a perfectly sound wink at the foot of Odelia's bed. Dooley likes to divide his time between my home and that belonging to Odelia's mom and dad. In other words, his loyalties are divided between his own human and Odelia, who is probably the more responsible of our pet parents. Though Odelia's mom, Marge, isn't too shabby either.

"I just hope that Gran hasn't been shot," said Dooley, as he gave me a look of alarm.

"If you like, we can go and take a look," I suggested. "Though it's probably kids playing with a toy gun."

I have to say that it had sounded like a real gun, though, and not a toy alternative, since they don't make that much noise. And since we didn't want to wake up our humans, we decided to take a look for ourselves before we alerted Odelia and Chase.

Next to the bed, a second smaller bed had been placed, where Grace slept. At one point, she would get her own bedroom, but for now, she still enjoyed sleeping in her parents' bedroom. The sound of the gunshot must also have awakened her, for she yawned and stretched. "What was that noise?" she asked.

"We're not sure," I said. "But we think it was a gunshot."

"It was coming from Blake's Field," said Dooley.

"We're going to take a look," I added.

"I'll come with you," she said, and threw off her blanket.

"No, you're not," I said. "You will stay right here."

"But I want to come!" she insisted.

"It might be dangerous, Grace," I said.

"As long as I'm with you guys, there's no danger," she argued. "You will be my bodyguards, won't you?"

And since she is one of those people who likes to do as she says and do it now, she climbed down from her bed and padded in the direction of the door.

"At least wear some shoes," I said.

"And a coat!" Dooley added.

We hurried after her, and I wondered what else we could say to make her stay put. The last thing we needed was for Grace to get shot out there in Blake's Field. Even if it was just kids playing, the field definitely was not a place for her to hang out. She was too little and Dooley and I hardly qualified as bodyguards.

But since Grace does what Grace wants, we had no alternative but to follow her out of the house and then to the fence, where Chase has put a sort of stepladder to allow us to climb the fence and climb down the other side. He probably didn't think it would also give his daughter license to do the same thing. Without waiting for us to catch up, the little girl was already clambering over that fence with surprising agility, almost as if she had never done anything else her entire life.

"She's an expert climber, Max," said Dooley, admiration clear in his voice.

"I'll say," I said.

"No, I said," he said.

"It's an expression, Dooley. It means I agree with what you just said."

"Oh, right," he said, and hurried up and over that fence to make sure that Grace wouldn't get into all kinds of trouble.

I brought up the rear as I often do. I'm one of the heavyweight cats of this world, you see. Some people call me fat, but I would argue that it's simple genetics and that I was born with big bones. With some effort, I also made it over the fence, and when I arrived on the other side, it took me a moment to locate my friend and Grace. They had already ventured deeper into the weeds, and when I finally caught up with them, I saw they had reached the clearing in the center of the field. A shack had been built there, with a car wreck located next to it. It's mostly home to several colonies of mice, and also a colony of shrews and even a colony of ants, but when I looked closer, I saw that it wasn't mice or shrews or ants that were crawling all over the place but a larger species of creature.

"Rats!" said Dooley with dismay. "Max, look, it's rats!"

"I can see, Dooley," I assured him. There were indeed plenty of rats, and as we ventured a little closer still, I saw they were all sitting around an object that was lying on the ground. It was the body of a man, and as we took a good look at the man, I saw that he was familiar to us. It was none other than our next-door neighbor Kurt Mayfield!

Next to his body, a little doggie sat. It was Fifi, our good friend the Yorkshire terrier. She looked absolutely devastated, and had one paw draped over her human's chest, and the other brought up to her face to wipe her tears.

"Max! Dooley!" she cried. "Someone shot Kurt!"

So that was the gunshot we had heard. It wasn't kids, or a hunter hunting rabbits. It was someone taking a shot at the retired music teacher!

The rats had fled the moment we arrived, and a good thing, too, for they might have considered Kurt a nice meal and could have started nibbling at him, which is not what you want when you've just been shot.

"The blood must have attracted them," I said, pointing to our neighbor's blood-soaked shirt.

"Is he still alive?" asked Grace, who had also toddled up to the man and seemed unsure how to proceed.

"He's alive," said Fifi. She gave me a pained look. "I wanted to come and get you, but I was afraid to leave him alone with these rats. They were very mean to me, Max. They said I shouldn't stand in the way of a nice snack. And they also said there was enough for all of us and I was being selfish for not wanting to share!"

"We'll go and get Odelia and Chase," I told her. "Come on, Grace. Time to leave."

"I'll stay here," said Fifi, "and guard him, shall I?"

"You do that," I said.

And so we hurried back the same way we had come, to wake up our humans and make sure Kurt got the help he needed.

"Is he dead, Max?" asked Grace. "It's just that I've never seen a dead man."

"And nor should you see one," I told her. "At your age all you should see are the dolls you like to play with."

I could have kicked myself for allowing Grace to tag along. Though I also knew there was absolutely no way I could have stopped her. In that sense she had inherited her mother's stubbornness. One day she would make a great reporter—or cop—or both, like Odelia.

"I hope he won't die, Max," said Dooley. "Fifi would be devastated if he died."

"All the more reason to make haste," I urged.

We slammed into the bedroom, me panting up a storm, and Dooley and Grace still as light on their feet as they had been when we set out. One advantage was that when I jumped up on Odelia's chest, she immediately was wide awake. I may not be the fastest cat on the block, but I'm the best at waking people up through the judicious application of the force of gravity.

"Max," she groaned sleepily. "How many times have I told you not to sit on my chest?"

"It's Kurt," I said, not wasting any more time. "He's been shot."

Immediately, she was wide awake, and sat up with a jerk. I fell to the floor and when she saw me, Dooley, and Grace looking up at her, she realized I wasn't kidding.

"Chase," she said urgently, as she elbowed her husband in the ribs. "Wake up. Kurt Mayfield has been shot."

It probably wasn't the best way to start our day. But it was a darn sight better than Kurt's start. I just hoped he would live. For Dooley was right: if he died, Fifi would be devastated.

CHAPTER 4

Odelia hurried over to her neighbor's side, and when she crouched down instantly knew it was bad. Kurt had been shot in the chest, and blood had spread across his shirt.

"We need to get him an ambulance," she said as she checked his vital signs. He was breathing, but shallow, and his pulse was weak.

"Way ahead of you, babe," said Chase as he held up his phone. "Ambulance should be here in five minutes." He glanced around. "Too bad this field is so overgrown that it's impossible to see a thing. The shooter could be hiding and watching us right now."

"I doubt it," said Odelia. "He won't be sticking around. Not unless he's a crazy person."

Chase gestured to Kurt. "If this isn't the work of a crazy person, I don't know what is. What do the cats say?"

"They didn't see anything. Though Fifi might have," she said as she cast a glance at the little doggie seated next to her human's body. She turned to Max. "Did Fifi see what happened?"

"She didn't," said Max. "She was playing nearby and came straight over when she heard the shot. But by then the shooter had already fled. She thinks he ran that way."

"I wonder if it was the same man who threatened Gran with a knife last night," said Dooley.

She stared at the little fluffy cat. "A man threatened Gran with a knife?"

"Gran was sleepwalking again last night," said Dooley. "I followed her, just like I do every night. Only this time she came here and sat on this bench to feed the birds, even though there weren't any birds around. She was also singing a song," and then, much to her surprise, he sang in a very soft and sweet voice, *"Feed the birds. Feed the birds. Tuppence a bag. Tuppence a bag."* He smiled. "I didn't know she could sing so well."

"Tell me about the guy with the knife," she insisted, figuring they could get to the part where Gran had been sleepwalking later.

"A man had been watching her from behind that tree over there. Then he walked straight up to Gran with a big knife, and for a moment I thought he was going to hurt her. But since she didn't see him, he seemed to relax, and then he disappeared again."

"Christ," she said, and glanced up at her husband. "My grandmother has been sleepwalking. And last night she was right here and a guy with a knife was also here."

"Could it have been the same guy?" asked Chase.

She shrugged. "Hard to tell. I think we'd better have this entire area searched."

He nodded and took out his phone again. If he called in the cavalry now, they might catch this guy before he did any more damage. Clearly, this sounded like the work of a madman. Why else would anyone threaten an old lady with a knife and shoot Kurt?

"Grace was also here," said Max. He looked a little sheepish. "She saw what happened to Kurt. I'm sorry!" he added when she gave him a look of exasperation. "We couldn't stop her!"

"No, I know," she said. Grace had a mind of her own, and when there was something she felt she needed to do, nothing could get in her way.

"I better get back to the house," she said. "Can you wait here for the paramedics, babe?"

Chase nodded. "I'll coordinate the search party. You take care of Grace."

She hurried back past the brambles and through the shrubberies to the house. She hated leaving Grace alone for too long, even though she had locked the door and made sure she couldn't get out this time. It was the only way to keep her from wandering off. When were they ever going to learn to lock the doors at night? Not only to keep the bad guys from coming in but also to keep their little girl from going on adventures.

She found Grace sitting on the couch eating a piece of toast. She looked happy as a clam, but then she usually did when she was left to her own devices. She picked her daughter up into her arms and looked her deep into her eyes. "Did you see the man wounded in the field, honey?"

The little girl nodded.

"He was hurt by a bad man," she explained. "But not to worry. The doctor is with him now, and he will be all right."

Grace nodded again and stuffed another piece of toast into her mouth.

"Can you promise me not to wander off again like that? There are dangerous people out here, you see, and Momma and Daddy don't like it when you wander off."

She stared at her with a sort of mulish expression on her face, and Odelia knew that she didn't agree with this last part at all. But that couldn't be helped. If she was going to have to worry every time she left Grace alone even for five seconds —or at night when she and Chase were asleep—she wouldn't have a life anymore.

Good thing the cats had been with her. They would never let anything happen to her.

She started preparing breakfast for herself, Grace, and also Chase—he would pick it up when he had a moment to spare—and as she was buttering a piece of toast, wondered who would get it into their head to shoot Kurt Mayfield? The man had never done anyone any harm. All she could think was that either he had come upon a crazy person with a gun or he had seen something he shouldn't have.

But what?

She knew that the field was often used by kids doing God knows what. And there were rumors that drug addicts had also discovered the place and enjoyed the relative peace and quiet from prying eyes it gave them. So far she hadn't noticed anything like that, but some of their neighbors had. Which is why the request to have the field turned into a park was echoing louder and louder throughout the entire neighborhood.

She handed her little girl another piece of toast, this time buttered and with strawberry jam, which was her favorite. She put it in her mouth with relish, and Odelia smiled. If she was traumatized by what she had seen, she certainly didn't give any indication. Maybe she hadn't seen much. The cats would have shielded her from whatever was out there as much as possible.

Max and Dooley now came traipsing in through the pet flap.

"What news?" she asked.

"Nothing yet," said Max. "Except that the ambulance has arrived and they've taken Kurt to the hospital."

"Will he be all right?" she asked.

"They seem to think so," said Max.

"Fifi must have smelled whoever did this to Kurt," said Dooley. "So maybe she can simply follow her nose and point this person out to you and Chase?"

She thunked her head, leaving butter on her forehead. "Of course, I hadn't thought of that! Thank you, Dooley."

Fifi had smelled the shooter, and she would be extra motivated to find him for them. "Okay, let me finish buttering this piece of toast," she said, "and then I'll go out there again and you guys can talk to Fifi and maybe tell her what you just told me, all right?"

Dooley gave her a sad look. "We already asked her, and she said she isn't sure she will be able to find him. She said he smelled really strange. Like… bleach?"

"He probably washed his clothes in bleach or something," said Max.

"So she won't be able to sniff him out or she will?" she asked.

"She said she will give it a shot, but she couldn't make any promises."

"She did say that she thought it was a man."

"Are you sure?"

"He smelled like a man," said Dooley.

She had finished preparing breakfast, and decided to quickly jump into the shower now that she had the chance. She had a feeling it was going to be a long day.

CHAPTER 5

*L*onnie Love checked his watch. He had been standing on the corner of the street for what felt like ages, and still that silly mutt wouldn't move along. But since he was a firm believer in letting the dog lead the way, he didn't give Raxo's leash a yank to encourage the Rottweiler to move along. As the country's most famous dog whisperer, he couldn't be seen in public going against his own philosophy. That would destroy the reputation he had built up over the years. And so he impatiently waited for Raxo to finish examining the spot on the wall where another dog must have previously done their business. Finally, after what felt like ages, the big Rottweiler lifted his hind leg and deposited a tiny tinkle at the very same spot. Then, with an air of satisfaction, he moved along, Lonnie following.

A couple of passersby did a double-take when they saw him walking Raxo and immediately took out their phones for a selfie with the famous television personality. He took it all in stride, as he knew it was par for the course when your face was on TV. He smiled at the camera and held up Raxo to pose for the couple, who said they'd post it on their Instagram. He told them to add the right hashtags, and then he was off. About twenty yards on, Raxo must have discovered another interesting spot he felt he needed to examine, for he paused once again, and the whole routine started from the beginning.

He ground his teeth but couldn't do anything about it. Back home in Switzerland, where he now lived, his assistant walked the dog, but since he was staying in his old home town of Hampton Cove for a couple of days, he had no other choice but to do it himself. Between Raxo being Raxo and several fans wanting selfies, it took him about an hour to cover the distance that separated the home that had once belonged to his parents from the hotel where he needed to be for his next appointment.

Taking Raxo along for his meeting was a risk, but that couldn't be helped. He arrived there just in time for the meeting, and only because he had picked the Rottweiler up in his arms and carried him to the hotel. Otherwise it might have taken another hour.

His contact was already waiting for him in the hotel bar. They selected a booth where they wouldn't be disturbed, and he told Raxo to lie at his feet and not be a nuisance. The dog was well-trained and knew from the tone of his master's voice that under these circumstances there was to be no funny business. Lonnie had asked the waiter for a bowl of fresh water for the dog and that should suffice for now. He also ordered a glass of chilled Chablis Premier Cru for himself, and then they got down to brass tacks.

"Did you bring it?" he asked.

The man, who was older than he had expected but still had all of his teeth and all of his hair, as he didn't fail to point out during the opening stages of the conversation, dug into his jacket pocket and took out a small black velvet bag. He placed it on the table, and Lonnie immediately snatched it up and hid it in the palm of his hand. He glanced around nervously, and when he was convinced that the coast was clear, quickly opened the bag and was pleasantly surprised to find inside it the trinket he had been looking for.

"Amazing," he said as he studied the precious little bauble. "Where did you find it?"

"That would be telling," said the guy. "Let's just say it took me quite a lot of work." He wiggled his eyebrows meaningfully, and Lonnie understood what he was referring to. And so he handed the man a wad of cash under the table. His counterpart turned to face the window and quickly counted the money. He smiled with satisfaction. "Always a pleasure to do business with you, Mr. Love."

"No names please," he implored.

"Of course. Discretion is key in this business, isn't it?" He leaned forward, glanced around, and whispered, "I've got another little trinket that might be of interest to you."

"What is it?" he asked as he watched the waiter approach with the Chablis.

The man shushed while the waiter hovered around the table for a moment, and then took off again. "It's a silver pendant," said the man. "That used to belong to none other than Eva Braun herself."

He gaped at the guy. "Eva Braun? Are you sure?"

The man displayed a grin. "I have it on good authority that it's the genuine article. The real deal. It's engraved with her initials. She used to wear it on her evenings out with the boyfriend. Rumor has it he gave her the pendant for her thirtieth birthday."

He sucked in a breath. "Not... the sea pearl and diamond pendant?"

"One and the same," the guy assured him.

"Do you have it?" he asked, excitement suddenly making him feel light-headed.

"I don't have it yet, but I know where I can get it," said the guy. "It was discovered quite by accident, and the person who's the owner doesn't even know what he has."

"How soon can you get it?" he asked eagerly.

"Just say the word, and I'll get to work."

"When?"

"Give me two weeks."

"Two weeks is too long," he said. "I'll be back in Switzerland by then."

"I could try and get it to you in a week," the man suggested. "But that means the price will go up, since I'll have to take more risk. The thing is that two weeks from now the couple who own the trinket will take a vacation. Right now, they're home, and to break in means a chance of being caught."

"So? Don't you have ways of dealing with such a contingency?"

The man grinned. "What do you think? Of course I have ways. But like I said, the price will go up because there's always a risk of getting caught. And the last thing I need is to get caught pocketing Miss Braun's pendant. Not when nobody knows what it is."

The guy was right. The moment he was caught with the pendant, it might be revealed that it was worth a fortune to a discerning collector like Lonnie. It might end up in the hands of another collector and never seen again. Or at a museum, with all of their security measures, making it a lot more complicated to lay his hands on it.

"Do what you can," he said. "And I'll reward you accordingly. In fact," he said, still feeling giddy about the discovery of the one item he'd always wanted to lay his hands on. "Get it for me this week, and I'll double your fee."

The man almost choked on his drink. "You have got to be kidding."

He gave him a serious look. "I never kid," he assured him.

CHAPTER 6

*P*inkie watched as the crowd shuffled by. As the loyal and loving dog belonging to museum guard Harold Hudspith, she had discovered that contrary to most members of her species, she actually liked it best when there were lots and lots of people paying a visit to the museum. The worst days were when there was nobody visiting the pieces that were on display and Harold just sat there feeling sad. Harold loved his job, and he liked it most when he got to interact with the visitors and explain things to them about the items on display. Today was a good day, though, for the Kirsten Gilmartin Museum was going through one of its best weeks. And it was all because of an exhibition of Nazi art, on loan from a Berlin museum. Some of the paintings had been created by none other than the Nazi führer himself, and attracted a lot of attention from across the state.

Harold was in his element, and when Harold was happy, Pinkie was happy—it was as simple as that. If he was sad, she was sad. Her mood mimicked his exactly, and that's the way it had been since he had saved her on a cold, dark night from a blizzard that had threatened to freeze her to death after a callous family had left her to die in the forest.

One of Harold's hobbies was taking long walks in the woods when he wasn't working, and that was what had saved her. He had come upon the nest which contained not only herself but also her six brothers and sisters and had brought them to the Rose Clinic, which dealt with sick and dying pets. And since he must have seen something in her, he decided to adopt her himself. They had been inseparable since, and he took her to work with him every day, where she kept him company, spending time in her basket, located on top of the radiator, just the way she liked it. She could never have it warm enough. Harold knew this and made sure she was always nice and snug.

She watched as he explained to an old couple how the collection had traveled all the way from Germany to Hampton Cove—a rare feat, as the museum was quite tiny when compared to some of the bigger museums, and still they had managed this major coup.

The museum wasn't Harold's, of course, he just worked there, but that had never stopped him from adopting a sort of proprietary pride in whatever was on display. And if the museum was doing well, it owed this to a large extent to the likes of Harold, who tirelessly worked to make its visitors feel at home.

Pinkie closed her eyes. It was on days like today that she felt most proud. Proud of Harold but also of the role she had played in the man's renaissance. Rumor had it that he hadn't been exactly on top of the world when he had gone for that walk in the woods on that fateful January morning. His wife had just passed away, and Harold had been feeling very down. Some people even said he had plans to end his life. And if he hadn't come upon that nest of screaming puppies, he just might have gone ahead with his plan. So in a sense, he had saved Pinkie, but she had also saved him. Which was probably why they were inseparable. She slept on Harold's bed at night and greeted him by rubbing his face in the morning. They spent all day at the museum together, and in the evenings, she traveled home with him on his bike, with her seated in a basket up front. And if it was cold outside, he bundled her inside his jacket and took her home that way.

In other words: they were the perfect team.

She looked up when a sort of argument seemed to have broken out. Harold was raising his voice, something he never did, and was yelling at a museum guest. It was a man with long dark hair and sunglasses, and he looked a little weird, Pinkie thought, dressed in a black leather jacket that extended all the way to the ground and army boots.

And then, as she watched on in horror and shock, all of a sudden the guy took out a shotgun from underneath that long jacket and aimed it at Harold!

"No!" Pinkie cried as she watched the terrible scene unfold.

A second man now also took out a gun and started waving it wildly at those present in the museum room, ordering them all to go and line up against the wall. A third man now removed a large sledgehammer from underneath his own long raincoat and started assaulting one of the display cases that held some nice pieces of jewelry. A fourth, fifth and sixth man did the same with some of the other display cases, and before long, the glass splintered, and the gangsters started snatching up the pieces, grabbing them from amongst the broken glass and shoving them into bags as they moved from display case to display case, smashing every single one and relieving them of their contents.

Harold, meanwhile, stood with his arms raised, looking as shocked and appalled as Pinkie herself did. The two men with the guns were waving them in a menacing fashion,

PURRFECT HEIST

instructing the visitors and Harold to stay put while their colleagues did the dirty work.

An alarm had started blaring, and security must have been triggered when the display cases were breached. It wouldn't be long before the people from the security company the museum had engaged would descend on the scene, and also the police.

The crooks knew this, which is why they worked so fast. The whole thing seemed to last a lifetime, but in actual fact, probably only took minutes from the moment the men had revealed their foul intentions to the moment they took off with the loot.

They escaped through a side entrance, and when security arrived, were long gone.

Harold lowered his arms. He looked brokenhearted, Pinkie saw, but also angry. Very angry. The museum was his life, and when you hurt the museum, you hurt Harold.

The police arrived soon afterward, and as the officers started combing the area and talking to witnesses, Pinkie could have told them that they were wasting their time. The crooks had fled, and judging from the way they perfectly executed their nefarious plan, this was a well-prepared heist and by now they were long gone—never to be found.

Harold also knew this, for he told the police officer who took his statement that there was probably very little hope that they would see the stolen works of art ever again.

It also meant that the museum would take a major reputational and possibly also financial hit. All in all, it was a major blow to Harold, and consequently to Pinkie.

Which is when she remembered that one of the members of cat choir was a cat named Max, and he was rumored to be a detective. She now wondered if she shouldn't ask Max to look into this business with the heist. For when she saw the sad look on Harold's face, she knew she had to do something. To save the museum, and to save Harold's job.

If the place closed down because of the robbery, Harold would be out of a job—a job he loved. And that was a lot worse than the loss of a few paintings and some jewelry.

And so, for perhaps the first time since Harold had brought her home, she decided to go on an adventure. She had to find Max and ask him to help Harold and the museum.

She glanced over her shoulder as she tiptoed out the door. Harold was still busy talking to the officer and didn't notice that she was leaving. He would be sad when he discovered her gone, but he wouldn't be sad for long. Not when she returned with Max.

CHAPTER 7

Lindsey Elford had seen the whole thing from her window, which looked out on Blake's Field. She had seen Kurt Mayfield walking his dog Fifi, the way he did every morning and every night. She had seen Kurt being accosted by a strange man, and she had even seen the man shoot Kurt without warning. The moment the shot rang out, and Kurt went down, her heart had skipped a few beats. She had never seen a man being shot before. Her hand had been on her phone the moment it happened, and she had been in contact with the police almost before Kurt's body hit the ground.

At first they didn't believe—that infernal Dolores always thought she knew better—but when she supplied plenty of details—like the fact that Fifi, Kurt's Yorkshire terrier, had guarded the body of her master, and that as she and Dolores spoke, two cats and a little girl had descended on the scene, both the cats and the little girl belonging to Odelia Poole and that husband of hers—Dolores had thanked her for getting in touch. Then she promptly hung up, causing Lindsey to stare at her phone. Time that Alec Lip hired a different dispatcher, she thought, for this one had definitely outstayed her welcome!

She wondered who could possibly be interested in taking a shot at Kurt Mayfield. Not that there was any great love lost between herself and the retired music teacher. Every time she met the guy, he was less than friendly or neighborly. In fact, it probably wasn't too much to say he was a curmudgeon—the neighborhood's very own Ebenezer Scrooge. Though ever since he had found love in the arms of Gilda Goldstein, he seemed to have softened a little bit. These days he sometimes even smiled at her when their paths crossed, which was quite the improvement. He had a lovely smile, it had to be said, and if only he would lighten up, he might be well on his way to becoming an actual human being and possibly even a cherished member of the neighborhood.

"Morris," she said urgently.

"What is it?" asked Morris. Her husband was in the bathroom shaving. He came out now, the left half of his face still covered in shaving cream.

"Kurt's been shot," she said, and pointed at the field. "Over there."

"Kurt? Shot? Are you sure?"

He sounded as shocked and surprised as she was. Things like that simply didn't happen in their part of the world. There were no gangs as far as she could tell, just regular families with kids and pets. Definitely no violent crime of any kind. Until now.

"Did you call the police?"

"I just got off the phone with Dolores. She didn't believe me at first," she scoffed.

"She better believe you. Maybe we should go and take a look? See what we can do?"

"We better stay out of this, Morris. Unless you want this killer to take a pop at us?"

"Is he still there? Where did he go?"

"He fled that way," she said, and pointed to the street that lined the field. "He had a car parked at the corner and he jumped in and took off."

"What did he look like?"

She shook her head. "He was too far away."

"But it was definitely a man?"

"I think so. He moved like a man."

"Maybe Kurt upset someone? Could be trouble in the family. You hear about that sort of thing all the time. Maybe he doesn't get along with his in-laws."

"But he and Gilda aren't even married."

"Still. Knowing Kurt, he's capable of rubbing anyone the wrong way. You used to hate him for the longest time, didn't you?"

"I didn't *hate* him," she said defensively. If she wasn't careful, the police would accuse *her* of shooting the guy. She was already having second thoughts about calling it in. Knowing Dolores, she would probably send over a couple of officers to talk to her. Make her file an official report or something. As if she had the time for such nonsense.

They watched as police vehicles arrived at the scene, and also an ambulance, that bopped and ground its way down the field to the spot where their neighbor had been shot. The Kingsleys were there, of course, so she knew that Kurt was in good hands.

"I hope he will live. Poor Gilda. She really seems to like him a lot, doesn't she?"

Morris laughed. "You sound surprised."

"Well, Kurt is a hard man to love, Morris, we all know that."

"Yeah, I guess you're right," he said, and returned to the bathroom to finish his shave. "This neighborhood is going to the dogs," he yelled from the bathroom. "And fast!"

"It's all because of that field," she said. "It attracts all kinds of vermin—and not just the rodent kind."

Ever since the company that was going to transform the field into some kind of new development had downed tools and gone out of business over some scandal that she never fully understood, things had gone from bad to worse. She was pretty sure that kids used the field to deal and use drugs at night. Even though the people from the neighborhood still used the field to walk their dogs, it had become too dangerous, with people reporting that they had found needles by the old shack, and also evidence of other drugs being consumed. Before long, drug addicts would take up sojourn there permanently. It was especially bad for the kids that lived around the field.

"They should turn it into a park," she told her husband. "They've been talking about it long enough. Maybe they will finally put their money where their mouths are."

Charlene Butterwick, their mayor, was related to the Kingsleys and the Pooles and spent time with her in-laws often enough to be aware of the problems the field presented to the neighborhood. So why she didn't do something about it was anyone's guess.

"It's none of our business, honey," Morris said as he returned to the living room to stand at the window. He had washed his face and looked smoothly shaven and smelling of cologne. He placed an arm around her shoulder as they watched the frantic activity unfold across the street. The paramedics had placed Kurt on a stretcher and shoved him into the ambulance, and now they were off with a screaming siren, which told them that Kurt was still alive. Police were combing the scene for evidence of the crime that had been committed, and the cats and one dog were also looking around.

"I'll bet those pets will find the killer," said Lindsey. "They're very clever, aren't they?"

Rumors had been circulating in the neighborhood for years that Odelia's cats were extremely intelligent and resourceful and had even been instrumental in assisting her in solving several crimes. Lindsey didn't know whether to believe such rumors, but it was true that the cats and their friends were pretty much ubiquitous in their neighborhood, always prancing about and satisfying their curiosity.

Just then, the doorbell rang, and she rolled her eyes. "I knew that Dolores would send the cops to start harassing us."

Morris grinned. "When you call the police, don't complain when they come running, honey."

He turned to open the door, and when he returned, he had two officers in tow, just as she had expected. And so Lindsey sat down at the dinner table and told them all about what she had seen, leaving out no detail, however small—except maybe the way she felt about Kurt.

That was nobody's business but hers and Morris's.

CHAPTER 8

It was probably safe to say that Fifi was one traumatized little doggie, but she was also determined to get to the bottom of this horrible thing that had happened to her human. And so she set out to find the miscreant who had shot Kurt. Shell-shocked at first, she was now becoming seriously upset that anyone had the gall to shoot Kurt without preamble—and especially since he had never done anything to anyone!

We had roped in Rufus, our other neighbor's sheepdog, and Harriet and Brutus had also joined the search party, and together the six of us set out to follow the trail of the killer and find him—come what may.

"Like I said, he smelled of bleach," said Fifi. "But I'll try to pick up his scent regardless."

"Odd that a man would smell of bleach," said Dooley. "Is that a common perfume that humans like to use, Max?"

"No, as far as I know, bleach isn't typically considered a perfume, Dooley," I said. "More like a product to clean things."

"Maybe he was a very dirty man and he was trying to clean himself up?" my friend suggested.

We had followed Fifi, who was keeping her nose to the ground and cutting a straight path to the nearest street.

"I don't like bleach," said Rufus. "It irritates my nostrils. Whenever I smell bleach it removes my sense of smell for hours."

"Let's hope this doesn't apply to Fifi," said Harriet. "Or otherwise, this will be the shortest search party in the history of search parties, you guys."

We had followed the little Yorkie from a distance and had made it as far as the street when she seemed to pause.

"What is it?" I asked as we joined her.

"I'm not sure," she said. "But the trail kind of ends right here." She was pointing to the corner of the street, and I saw an oil puddle, where possibly a car had been parked.

"He probably got into his car and took off," I suggested.

"You're not going to be able to follow that car, are you, Fifi?" asked Rufus.

She shook her head sadly. "No, I don't think I will be able to follow that car."

"Okay, so what do we know?" I asked. "That a man walked up to Kurt and shot him point blank in the chest. Then he set out for his car and drove off. Oh, and he smells of bleach." I scratched my head. "That doesn't tell us a lot, does it?"

"Maybe there are people living on this street that have seen something," Brutus suggested. We glanced up at the houses that lined this particular part of the street, an entire row of which overlooked the field.

"Someone must have seen something," Harriet agreed. "And odds are that they will have called the police by now and put them on the trail of this killer."

Fifi grimaced. "He's not a killer until he's actually killed a person, Harriet," she pointed out. It was a sensitive subject, that much was clear. And that was no surprise: as long as Kurt survived, the person that had shot him wasn't a killer but a shooter. A minor difference, perhaps, and a matter of semantics, but to Kurt it was definitely a matter of life and death—quite literally.

And as we stood there, conferring as to how to proceed, suddenly a small dog of the Papillon variety walked up to us. She looked quite exhausted, I saw.

"Max?" she asked. "Are you Max the great detective, by any chance?"

"I am Max," I said. "And it's true that I do a little detecting from time to time."

Her face lit up with an expression of intense relief. "My human has been attacked," she said. "Or rather, the museum where he works has been attacked, and if we don't find the people responsible, he might lose his job. My name is Pinkie," she added, almost as an afterthought. She directed a pleading look at me. "Can you... can you help me, Max?"

I exchanged a glance with my friends. I could have told her that we were busy dealing with an urgent matter of our own, but she was looking at me so piteously that I couldn't get myself to utter the words and send her away.

So instead I said, "Tell us all about it, Pinkie. What exactly happened to your human?"

She perked up. "Well, Harold is a museum guard, you see. And now the museum has been robbed. The crooks came in and held everyone present at gunpoint while they attacked the display cases with sledgehammers and stole everything inside. Some very valuable pieces were in those display cases and now everything is gone. And since it's such a small museum this is going to put them out of business for sure.

And then Harold won't have a job anymore, and he's already in a precarious state because his wife died and and and…" She suddenly broke into tears, and I think we all felt for her.

"Don't cry, Pinkie," said Dooley consolingly. "Max will help you. He will find these people and he'll make sure every last piece that was stolen is returned. Won't you, Max?"

"Um…"

"Won't you, Max?" he insisted.

"Well, I'll do my best, of course," I said.

Brutus grinned. "Did you just take on another case, Maxie baby?"

"No, *I* did not," I corrected him. "*We* all took on another case, Brutus."

His face sagged. "Of course we did."

"If you like, I'll also help," said Fifi. "My human was shot, but that doesn't mean I can't be of assistance elsewhere. And besides, it will take my mind off things while Kurt is in the hospital."

"Your human was shot?" asked Pinkie.

Fifi nodded. "Just now. So I can relate to what you're going through, Pinkie."

"My human was held at gunpoint," said Pinkie. "But at least he wasn't shot. Oh, that's so terrible, Fifi."

"I know. But Kurt is strong. I'm sure he will survive."

"Let's hope so," said Rufus. "And if he doesn't, you can always come and live with us, Fifi," he said.

Fifi smiled. "That's very kind of you, Rufus. But I'm not sure if Ted and Marcie will agree. They might not like little doggies like myself."

"They will like it or I will elope," said Rufus with a frown.

"I don't think that will be necessary," said Fifi, holding up a tiny paw. "Like I said, Kurt is a strong man. He will live." I got the impression she was saying it more to convince herself than because she actually believed it, and that was fine with me. Better to stay positive and focus on Kurt getting better.

"Okay, so better show us to your museum," I told Pinkie.

And so we were off after Pinkie, leading the way.

It was certainly shaping up to be one interesting day!

CHAPTER 9

Vesta didn't like this. She didn't like it one bit. A shooting? On her block? And she, as the leader of the neighborhood watch, hadn't even been informed? This was an outrage, pure and simple. By the time she was told, the whole thing was over, police scouring the scene and Kurt in the hospital fighting for his life.

"I don't get it," said Marge as she took a sip from her morning coffee. "Why shoot Kurt Mayfield, of all people? He may not be the nicest man around, but when has not being nice ever been a reason to get shot?"

"Kurt will be fine," said Tex. "He's one of those guys who will always be spared by life."

"And how do you figure that?" asked Marge. "He wasn't spared now, was he? Shot in broad daylight, and so close to his home, too," she added, as if that was the worst part of it.

"They should have informed me," said Vesta, not for the first time. "A shooting on my block and they didn't even think about telling the leader of the neighborhood watch. It just goes to show how little the police care about the kind of work we do."

"Oh, that reminds me," said Marge as she put down her cup. "Dooley told us you went walkabout again last night? And this time you went all the way out to the field?"

"Did I? I don't recall," she said. Dooley had spread these rumors before, and frankly, she didn't believe any of it. The cat was simply making things up as far as she could tell.

"You shouldn't be out there by yourself in the middle of the night, Ma," said Marge. "It's dangerous. You can see now for yourself, what with Kurt being shot."

"It's all this neighborhood watch business," said Tex. "Being out there all night, every night. And then when you stay in you start sleepwalking. At your age you shouldn't be out there anyway. Leave this stuff to the police. They get paid to make sure the streets are safe, not you. Plus, they're trained professionals who know how to handle themselves."

"Well, I just happen to feel responsible for the safety of my fellow Hampton Covians," she said. The one night she had decided to stay home and go to bed early, and now Dooley was claiming she had been sleepwalking. "And besides, there's absolutely no truth to this. Dooley is seeing things. He probably had a bad dream and now he's telling these tall tales about me wandering off in the middle of the night. It didn't happen, all right?"

"He also said that there was a man last night," said Marge. "A man with a knife. And that you were feeding the birds when in actual fact you were feeding the rats." She shivered. "I really don't want you out there by yourself again, Ma. I'm going to put a gate at the top of the stairs." She turned to her husband. "Can you install a gate at the top of the stairs, honey? Make sure Ma doesn't wander off again?"

"A gate!" she cried. "What am I? A toddler? If you dare install a gate I'll file a complaint for elder abuse."

"We're just trying to keep you safe," said Marge soothingly. "Especially if it's true that a man with a knife was out there with you last night." She brought a distraught hand to her face and her eyes went wide. "Oh, my God! What if it was the same man who shot Kurt? Maybe it's a bum living in the shack. It happened before, remember?"

Oh, did she remember? It had been a dark and stormy night, and the bum living out there by himself had moved into their home for the time being, to weather the storm. Fortunately for them, he hadn't been a violent man. Or at least not overly so.

She took a sip from her coffee and thought about her daughter's words. With all the details that Dooley had supplied, it was hard to imagine he had dreamed it all up. Dooley was a sweet and naive cat, but he wasn't a fantasist by any stretch of the imagination. "Are you sure I was out there?" she asked.

"Absolutely. And it wasn't the first time, though on previous occasions Dooley says you didn't wander off too far. Three nights ago you ate a pork chop. And it's true, because in the morning that pork chop was gone. I figured it was the cats, but it was you. And two nights ago you ate all the leftover pancakes. All of them. Gone!"

"I do get hungry at night," she admitted. "But why would I go out to Blake's Field and feed the birds?"

"Sleepwalkers often do things that later they don't remember," said Tex. "It's only natural that you wouldn't know what happened."

"Good thing Dooley followed you or we would never have known," said Marge as she got up from the breakfast table.

"Maybe we should get you to a sleep lab," Tex suggested. "They could do a nocturnal sleep study. A polysomnography. They monitor your brain waves while you sleep, the oxygen level in your blood, heart rate, breathing, eye and leg movements. It could give us an idea of what's going on. There could be an underlying medical condition."

"Good idea," said Marge. "And maybe put her on some kind of medication. Make sure it doesn't happen again."

"I don't need no stinkin' medication!" she cried, getting up from the table and shoving her chair back with some force. "No gate and no medication and most definitely no sleep lab! I'm not a toddler and I'm not a guinea pig for your weirdo experiments!"

And with these words, she stomped out of the kitchen. Who did they think they were to order her about like that? If they kept this up she would move out and go and live with Scarlett—simple as that. Though as she set foot for the back fence and started climbing over, she vaguely seemed to remember she had done this exact thing before—and not so long ago either. So what if she *had* ventured out there last night? She must have had a perfectly good reason, even if she didn't remember.

She arrived at the old shack and, judging from the police activity, things were still in progress. She saw Abe Cornwall pottering about, and members of his team of crime investigators collecting trace evidence from the scene where Kurt had been shot. She also saw Chase and Odelia discussing things with Alec, and so she waved at them to get their attention. When that didn't work, she yelled, "Hey! Alec! What's going on?"

Alec made a face and came wandering over. "You shouldn't be here, Ma," he said.

"And why not?" she said indignantly. "I'm the leader of the neighborhood watch so I have every right to be here. Now are you going to tell me what's going on or do I have to start my own investigation?"

He held up his arms. "There's no need for that, Ma. Kurt Mayfield was shot early this morning while walking his dog.

Of the shooter there's no trace. A neighbor who saw the whole thing said it was probably a man, dressed in black and obscuring his features with a hoodie. He shot Kurt at point blank range in the chest and then fled the scene."

"This neighborhood is going to the dogs, and fast," she said. "Drug deal gone wrong, you think? Kurt and his dealer not getting along?"

"Kurt is not a drug addict, as far as we know," said Alec.

"It's the quiet ones that are always the worst," she told her son. She wagged a finger in his face. "Never be deceived by appearances, Alec. Kurt has probably been buying drugs off this guy for years, and now they fell out for some reason, and the dealer shot him. End of story."

But Alec was shaking his head. "Please keep your theories to yourself, Ma. And whatever you do, don't get involved in my investigation, is that understood? That means you're not to talk to any witnesses and you're not to come anywhere near Kurt or any member of his family, all right? And I'll hold you to that." And with these words, he returned to his meeting with Chase and Odelia—who for some reason were allowed to be involved in the investigation while she was not.

It wasn't fair, she felt. Not fair at all!

But then she was of an age where she knew that life wasn't fair. But that didn't mean she had to like it!

And so she stomped back in the direction of the house and took out her phone to put in a call to her neighborhood watch second-in-command. "Scarlett? We've got a case."

Nobody could tell her what to do—especially not that busybody son and daughter of hers—who did they think they were? She would teach them a thing or two about running an investigation. She would collar the guy who shot Kurt long before they did!

CHAPTER 10

We had been walking for a little while and attracting a lot of attention when we arrived at the museum where Pinkie's human worked. The place was locked down by the presence of plenty of police officers who had descended on the scene. Police cars stood idling at the curb, their lights flashing, and it was clear that something dramatic had happened here.

The Kirsten Gilmartin Museum, so called after a patron of the arts who had donated her entire private collection and set up the museum, was a smallish affair, as museums go, housed in a low-slung hacienda-style villa. Not exactly the Guggenheim, but then one doesn't expect a monstrosity like that in a small town like Hampton Cove. It was still a pretty popular museum with the tourist crowd and attracted a lot of visitors, especially in the summer months. Though the fact that it had a great air conditioning system might have something to do with that. When tourists get too overheated from lying on the beach, they like to spend some time in a cool museum looking at fine art.

"So what was stolen, exactly?" I asked as we looked for a way in.

"Well, everything from the exhibit that was targeted," said Pinkie. "Nazi art."

"Nazi art?" I asked, surprised that a thing like that even existed.

"Yes, paintings by Adolf Hitler and other stuff belonging to members of his regime," said Pinkie. "It was attracting a lot of attention and has been touring through Europe for the past five years before arriving in the States. After this exhibition closed, it was going to move to the big city. Though now that everything has been stolen…" She sighed deeply. "So you see, even if the insurance pays out, it's not going to make any difference. These pieces are irreplaceable, and it was the responsibility of the museum to keep them safe—the responsibility of Harold, in fact, who's in big trouble now."

"They can't possibly blame Harold for this," I said. "Any museum can be hit by a gang of robbers, and if they had guns there was nothing that Harold could do."

"Probably better that he didn't do anything," said Brutus. "They might have shot him if he tried to interfere."

"They were armed to the teeth," Pinkie agreed. "And they held us all at gunpoint until their colleagues were done smashing the display cases and grabbing paintings from the walls and stealing everything they could lay their hands on."

Pinkie had shown us a side entrance that was only used by personnel and led us in. We slipped between the legs of a police officer who stood drinking a cup of coffee and munching on a donut, and soon the intrepid little Papillon led us to the room where it had all gone down. The place was a mess, with glass on the floor and all of the display cases having been smashed to pieces. She was right that nothing had been left, and that the thieves had really gone to town on the place. We walked through to the next room, and I saw that here nothing had been taken. "Looks like you're right," I said. "They specifically targeted this section of the collection, leaving the rest untouched."

"Maybe they were fans of Hitler?" Dooley suggested. "And wanted to collect some of his memorabilia?"

"How many were there?" I asked.

"Six," said Pinkie. "Two were holding us at gunpoint while four others went from display case to display case and destroyed them with sledgehammers and then grabbed everything and put it in big bags. The whole thing only lasted minutes."

"How horrible," said Fifi as she put her nose to the ground and sniffed. Rufus, watching her, followed suit. Finally, she frowned. "I smell bleach again."

"Same here," said Rufus, and sneezed. He wrinkled up his nose. "I hate bleach."

"Bleach?" I asked. "How odd. Same as with Kurt."

"Could it have been the same gang?" asked Brutus.

Fifi shook her head. "Bleach is bleach, Brutus. It all smells exactly the same. Though it's quite a coincidence, wouldn't you say?"

"It sure is," I said. "When exactly did this heist take place?"

"Um…" Pinkie glanced at a big clock that was suspended over the door. "The museum had just opened its doors, so there weren't a lot of people present yet. Maybe five or six. So it must have been just past eight? Something like that."

"And Kurt was shot at seven," I said. "So it's possible that the person who shot him was part of the gang that hit the museum one hour later. I mean, I don't see the connection between a shooting in Blake's Field and this heist, but we can't rule it out."

"So what do you think?" asked Pinkie, giving me a hopeful look. "Any ideas, Max?"

She seemed to think I was some kind of savant and that I

simply had to take one look at the crime scene and immediately be able to identify the perpetrators, know that one of them had a hairy wart on his upper left buttock and what they had for dinner last night. But that wasn't how it worked. "I'm sorry, Pinkie. But right now, I don't know who did this to your human. But I can promise you that I will do my best for you, all right?"

She seemed slightly disappointed, but must have realized that her expectations had been a little inflated. I don't know what stories people had told her about me, but I could have pointed out to her that I'm not a miracle worker. More like the plodding kind of detective who has to sift through the evidence and take his time to find things out.

"Look, it's Chase," said Dooley as he pointed at the entrance to the room. He was right. And the cop was accompanied by Odelia. They must have made the short trek over just after we had set out from Blake's Field. They looked quite surprised to see us, and Odelia immediately came over.

"What are you guys doing here?" she asked.

"Pinkie here belongs to Harold Hudspith," I explained. "The museum guard? She's asked us to look into this heist for her."

She smiled. "I should have known that you were one step ahead of us, Max. So what have you found out?" She glanced around to make sure that nobody saw her communicating with us, for that would have raised all kinds of questions.

"Well, looks like there's a link between the heist and the shooting of Kurt Mayfield," I said. This surprised her greatly.

"What link would that be?"

"Both perpetrators smelled of bleach," I said. "And that's all we have right now. Except that the collection consisted of Nazi art, so the robbers had a special interest in that, apparently."

She nodded. "Yes, so we've been told." She gestured over

to her husband, who stood examining one of the smashed-up display cases closely. "We're just about to talk to the museum director. Want to sit in on the interview?"

"Absolutely," I said.

"Though maybe not all of you," she said. "Four cats and three dogs is a little much. He would think that we've gone mad. Maybe just you and Dooley, if that's all right."

Brutus made a face. "We're being excluded again, huh? I should have known."

"Always playing favorites," said Harriet.

"It's got nothing to do with playing favorites," said Odelia. "But with being practical. Maybe you guys could look around for possible clues, all right? Let's go, Max."

And so I followed Odelia, and so did Dooley.

Harriet and Brutus weren't happy about it, but that couldn't be helped. Odelia was right. She couldn't very well show up with an entire troupe of pets in tow. They'd think the circus was in town, not the Hampton Cove PD's top investigators.

"We'll find these robbers for you, Pinkie," I could hear Harriet say. "We don't need Max at all."

"But Max is the detective, isn't he?"

"*We're* the detectives," said Harriet.

"No, *we're* the detectives," said Fifi. "Rufus and I. Isn't that right, Rufus?"

"I guess so," said the big sheepdog, but he didn't sound all that convinced.

Looked like Pinkie had asked for one detective and instead she got an entire flock!

CHAPTER 11

The director of the museum was a little bearded and bespectacled man named Kelvin Stamper. He looked extremely sad over the tragedy that had befallen him. We met the man in his office, a tiny cubicle tucked away in a far corner of the museum.

"This is a tragedy," he said, throwing up his arms. "We had only just opened the exhibit and were anticipating a lot of interest from the community, and now this."

"We noticed that only one part of the collection was targeted," said Chase as he took a seat in front of the director's desk.

"Yes, the Nazi collection," said the director. "Officially called Art in the Third Reich. It has never traveled outside of Europe before. This was the first time it crossed the ocean, and now it's gone!" He buried his face in his hands, and actually burst into tears.

"Do you have any idea who could be behind this?" asked Odelia as she reluctantly continued their questioning of the director.

He looked up and wiped his eyes with a large white handkerchief. "No idea whatsoever," he said. "Though like I said, we were anticipating a lot of interest in this particular exhibit, since it's the first time it traveled outside of its home continent. There were some unique pieces in the collection, like artwork that was created by the Führer himself—original paintings by Adolf Hitler. That kind of thing naturally attracts a lot of attention. We had plenty of reporters and even camera crews during our opening night." He smiled at Odelia. "If I remember correctly, you were also here, Mrs. Kingsley."

"Yes, I did a big piece for the *Gazette*," she said. "And it struck me that the museum was pretty crowded on opening night."

"The biggest crowd we've ever drawn," said the director proudly, before collapsing again. "What am I going to tell the Berlin people? They were anticipating a successful tour of the major museums in the US, and now this. Everything gone!"

"Why did the Berlin people pick your museum?" asked Chase. "No offense, but yours isn't exactly the most prestigious or well-known museum in the country, Mr. Stamper."

"None taken," said the director. "Well, all I can say is what they told me. They wanted to have a trial at a smaller venue before they organized a tour of the bigger and more prestigious institutions. Gauge interest, you see. Though if what we saw here was any indication, their tour would have been a smash. Already they had several of the bigger museums express an interest. Even the Guggenheim wanted in on the bonanza."

"The major coup was for you, though," said Odelia. "Wouldn't you say?"

"Absolutely," said the museum director fervently. "This would have put us on the map." His face crumpled. "It will still put us on the map, but not in a good way. We might even have to close our doors after this."

"Is it a safe assumption that these robbers targeted your museum because your level of security wasn't on par with that of the bigger museums?" asked Odelia.

The man nodded mournfully. "Good security is expensive, and even though I had upped ours considerably, I couldn't possibly afford to hire extra people, even though that's what the Berlin curators were pressing for. I should probably have listened to them. Now they might press charges against us for negligence. Sue us into oblivion."

"Surely you were insured, though, right?"

"We *are* insured, and the collection itself is also insured, but no money can replace the items that were on display. These are unique pieces and some of them are literally invaluable, meaning that no price can be put on them. Like the art that was created by Adolf Hitler—it's impossible to quantify the damage that was done by stealing those pieces. They will be lost forever. An irreparable loss."

I would have told him that paintings by the leader of the Nazis weren't exactly a big loss, but clearly he thought differently about this sort of thing than a laycat like me.

"Okay, let's go over possible suspects," said Chase, taking out his notebook. "The museum hasn't received any threats in the days or weeks leading up to the opening?"

"Nothing," said the director.

"The Berlin museum, perhaps?"

"As far as I know, they haven't received any threats either," said the director. "And they've been showing this specific exhibition for thirteen years, and touring it across Europe for five years, so it's not as if it has suddenly come out of the blue. Though like I said, it is the first time that it has crossed the Atlantic. It was shown in many different museums in Europe. Holland, Austria, Portugal, Belgium…"

"But never any problems? Attempts to steal anything? Or destroy parts of the exhibit? Protests being staged?"

"Nothing of the kind," said the director. "Most people know better than to conflate displaying these types of exhibits with approving of the politics and ideology of the people who created these works of art." He shook his head. "The only thing I can think of is that a major collector of Nazi art saw this as an opportunity to expand his private collection with several unique pieces. Which means we'll never see them again."

"A private collector?" asked Odelia.

"Any idea who?" asked Chase.

The director shook his head. "There are several known collectors, but they are respectable people and would never engage in this kind of tomfoolery. But there are also those that are dead set on their privacy. They will bid at auctions through a third party or try to obtain items in all kinds of underhanded ways. Collecting Nazi art isn't the most glamorous or prestigious pastime, as you can probably understand, and so they prefer to remain anonymous—their interest strictly personal."

"Can you give us a list of names of the collectors you do know?" asked Chase.

"Of course. Though the people who created the exhibit will probably be more aware of these people than me. But I'll get you a list."

"There's one other matter we need to discuss," said Chase. "Sometimes these heists are an inside job. Meaning that a member of your staff or even your security may be involved."

But the director was shaking his head even before Chase had finished his sentence. "Absolutely not," he said adamantly. "Out of the question. I will vouch for every person on my staff."

"Even the security guy…" Chase checked his notes. "Um, Harold Hudspith?"

"Harold has been with me for thirty years," said the director. "I can vouch for him."

"You have to admit that he would be best placed to give these crooks the inside track. Best time to hit the museum and that sort of thing."

"You're barking up the wrong tree, detective. If Harold is involved in this somehow, I will eat my hat." He pointed to a nice specimen hanging from a coatrack in the corner of his office. I hoped he was right, for if he had to eat that, he'd have stomach trouble.

Chase and Odelia thanked him for his time, and we were off. So far we hadn't learned a lot, though the notion of a private collector of Nazi art ordering a hit on the museum was definitely an interesting one and was worth following up on.

We left the office and saw that we were being met by an attractive woman who desired speech with us, and when I say 'us' I mean Chase and Odelia. Very rare is the person who wants to talk to a pair of cats in connection with a museum heist. Not even Pinkie would get the benefit of a police interview, even though she was a witness.

"Detective Kingsley?" asked the woman. "Mildred Mildew. I represent the insurance company. Can I have a moment of your time?"

Well, that was quick, I thought. Though of course the insurance had a vested interest in finding that loot—probably even more than we did.

CHAPTER 12

Vesta met up with her friend Scarlett in the cafeteria of the senior center, where they proceeded to take their usual table near the window and Vesta poured her lament into her friend's ear. "They want to install a gate at the top of the stairs to prevent me from sleepwalking," she complained. "And they also want to send me to a sleep lab where they will run all kinds of tests on me, and give me medication, can you believe it?"

"But... have you been sleepwalking?" asked Scarlett.

She shrugged. "According to Dooley, I have. Though I can't remember a thing, so it's hard to know for sure. He claims that last night I was out in Blake's Field and I was feeding the birds while I was singing a song from *My Fair Lady*."

Scarlett laughed, and even Vesta had to crack a smile.

"I didn't even know I had remembered the song! I haven't seen that movie in years."

"Clearly it must have made a deep impression on you," said Scarlett as she took a sip from her latte macchiato—a nice change of pace from her usual cappuccino.

She raised her hand as Dick Bernstein came walking by. He smiled and brought his cup of coffee over to their table and took a seat. "And how are you ladies doing on this fine morning?"

"Not so fine," said Vesta. "My family is accusing me of sleepwalking, and now they want to lock me up."

Dick's handsome face clouded. "Never live with your family would be my advice. Before you know it, they will start drugging you and telling people that you've lost your mind. It happened to a good friend of mine. Now he's in an institution and he's drooling on a bib all day. I went to pay him a visit the other day and I didn't even recognize him. Well, he didn't recognize me either, but that's probably because of all the pills they're feeding him."

"I don't think Tex and Marge would go that far," said Vesta. "Would they?"

Dick frowned. "Never trust family," he said. "They're the worst people in the world when it comes to doing what's best for you. Can't you move in with Scarlett?"

Scarlett raised her finely penciled eyebrows. "That would be the end of *that* friendship," she said, and she was probably right. The only reason they got along so well was because they didn't live together. Once she moved in with Scarlett they would probably clash over all kinds of stuff. Like who got to use the bathroom first in the morning, who had to clean the toilet bowl and how to load the dishwasher. She knew from experience that living with other people carried its own set of difficulties and inevitably led to friction. Every time she found one of Tex's hairs in the sink she wanted to smack him in the face, and she knew he probably felt the same way about her.

"You could always move in with me," Dick suggested. "I have plenty of space."

It was certainly an appealing prospect. Rock Horowitz,

another good friend of theirs, walked into the cafeteria, and when he saw the small gathering, made a beeline for them and took a seat. "My goodness," he said. "Did you hear about the museum?"

"What museum?" asked Dick.

"The Kirsten Gilmartin! It was robbed this morning. Six men with guns held it up and took off with an entire collection of Nazi art."

"Nazi art?" asked Scarlett. "What is Nazi art?"

Vesta suggested, "Art that used to belong to Nazis?"

"Or that was created by Nazis, maybe?" said Rock.

"I'll tell you exactly what Nazi art is," said Dick. "Another good friend of mine is a collector, and he loves the stuff. Can't shut up about it, even though I have to say I feel uncomfortable looking at a bunch of paintings that were created by one of the worst monsters in human history."

"A friend of yours collects this stuff?" asked Vesta, much surprised.

"That's right. I try not to hold it against him. He's not a Nazi himself, of course, just into the type of art these people used to create. He's got three paintings that he claims were made by the Führer himself, though I have my doubts. I've looked it up online, and if you count the number of paintings in private collections and hanging in museums across the world, Hitler should have spent every waking moment of his life painting the stuff, and that simply wasn't the case. So plenty of those things are obvious fakes."

"Do you think your collector friend had something to do with this heist?" asked Vesta.

"Oh, I doubt it," said Dick. "He's not a criminal at all and acquired all of his paintings from reputable sources only."

"It's still a terrible thing," said Rock. "Especially for the director, who's a good friend of my sister's."

"Okay, so let's thrash this thing out," said Vesta, wanting

to get to the bottom of this once and for all. "If I come and stay with you, how would that work, exactly?"

Dick seemed surprised, then laughed. "I thought we were talking about the heist."

"Forget about the heist," she said. "I'm talking about my family wanting to lock me up in some sleep lab and have me drooling on my bib for the rest of my life."

"They wouldn't lock you up," said Scarlett. "Only keep you there overnight, to find out what's causing the sleepwalking."

"I spent a night in one of those sleep labs once," said Rock. "It wasn't a lot of fun, but it wasn't terrible either. And I did learn a lot about my sleeping habits. I've been wearing one of those apnea masks since then, and it's helped me sleep a lot better."

"Okay, so if I have to wear a sleeping mask I'd rather kill myself," said Vesta. When the others all laughed, she cried, "I don't want to wear one of those contraptions!"

"It's not that bad," said Rock. "It takes some getting used to, that's true, but once you do, it's actually quite nice. You will sleep so much better and feel rested in the morning."

"I won't have it on my face," she said. "I simply won't!"

"Oh, Vesta, you're too funny," said Dick as he wiped the tears from his eyes. "Okay, so think about it and let me know. There's always a room available for you at the house."

She knew that Dick lived in a pretty big place, and ever since his wife Amelia had left him to his own devices, he often felt that the house was too big for him. So he probably wouldn't mind the company. Then again, she couldn't imagine herself living with the guy. He would probably try to hit on her all the time. He simply couldn't help himself. It was one thing for Tex and Marge to install a gate at the top of the stairs to prevent her from tumbling down and breaking her neck, and willingly subjecting herself to Dick's flirtations on a continuous basis.

She got up and said, "I better get going. My neighbor has been shot, and I want to pay him a visit at the hospital."

"Your neighbor was shot?" asked Rock. "Which neighbor?"

"Kurt Mayfield," she said. "Shot this morning while he was walking his dog." She shook her head. "Right under the nose of the leader of the neighborhood watch, too. Drug deal gone wrong would be my best guess, but of course Alec wouldn't hear of it."

"I didn't know Kurt Mayfield was into drugs," said Dick.

"You'd be surprised by the number of people that are into drugs these days," said Rock. "Even people you least expect it from. I was having dinner at my sister's place the other night when I happened to walk in on my brother-in-law sniffing a suspicious-looking white powder off the bathroom sink, if you please!"

"My God," said Dick. "So what did you say?"

"I pretended I hadn't noticed, of course. What could I say?"

"You could have cut in," Dick quipped, but when the others didn't laugh, he held up his hands. "Not funny?"

"Not funny, Dick," said Scarlett.

"I know, I know. I'm sorry."

"I was shocked, of course, but when I told my sister, she denied it. Said I was seeing things. Which makes me think she's also a user. My own sister!"

"Terrible," said Vesta. "Absolutely terrible." It strengthened her belief that Kurt was a secret drug user and had fallen foul of his dealer. Now all she had to do was convince her son.

CHAPTER 13

"We have to find clues, Brutus!" said Harriet. "Clues! I mean, how hard can it be?"

She knew that a good detective's work was all about finding that killer clue. The one clue that rules them all. And so if she found it before anyone else did, she would be the hero of the hour and could show Odelia that there was only one detective worth their salt in this family and that detective was she.

"So what are we looking for, exactly?" asked Fifi.

"Yes, what does this clue look like?" asked Rufus. "Just to know what we're looking for, you know."

"If I knew what it looked like, I would have found it by now, wouldn't I?" she said. God, how hard was it to find a clue? And since she knew she couldn't rely on her assistants, no matter how well-meaning they might be, or willing to assist, she knew she would have to do it herself. And so she set out to find the clue that would tell her who exactly was behind this whole business with the heist.

Unhindered by the police, who were making sure that no one entered the museum but weren't too bothered with the ones that were already inside, she searched the floor of the room looking for a sign that could lead to the identity of the heisters—if heisters was the word she was looking for.

Brutus also joined her, and so did Fifi, Rufus, and even Pinkie, who was determined to save her human's career.

She had read somewhere that a detective always searches a crime scene according to a grid, and so she started in a corner of the room and made her way down to the other side, making sure that she covered every inch. By the time she was halfway through, she still hadn't found anything out of the ordinary. She had found a cigarette butt, but it was hard to know for sure if it belonged to the robbers or not. She still made a mental note to tell Odelia later on. Maybe she could extract DNA from the butt and that would break this case wide open. And she had almost reached the end of the line when she saw an odd object lying on the floor, hidden amongst the broken glass. It was an earbud of some kind. Like the cigarette butt, it was hard to know if it belonged to the heist perpetrators or not, but she still filed it away for later use. Odelia and Chase would have to do the rest of the work. After all, she couldn't be expected to do everything in their place.

She reached the end of the search and apart from the butt and the bud had nothing to show for it, and when she convened with the others, they hadn't found anything of note either. It was all very discouraging, she felt. And she knew that Max and Dooley would mock her if she didn't produce something tangible—something that constituted hard evidence that the people who had stolen those artifacts had left something of themselves behind. Locard's exchange principle, Max had once called it: every perp takes something from the crime scene but also leaves something behind that can reveal their identity.

But before she could go over the whole room again, Max

and Dooley returned, with Chase and Odelia right behind them. And so she told Odelia about the butt and the bud, and much to her surprise, she seemed extremely interested in her discovery. Chase even put both items in separate plastic evidence baggies, and Max told her what an amazing find she had made. It certainly buoyed her mood to a considerable extent.

"Why thanks, Max. So you see that you're not the only detective in this family."

"Of course I'm not the only detective, Harriet," the voluminous blorange cat said. "I never claimed I was. In fact, detective work is a team effort, and Odelia and Chase couldn't do it without all of our assistance, as the evidence that you found proves."

"It's a hearing aid," said Chase now as he studied the earbud closely.

"Hearing aid?" asked Odelia. "Do you think it belongs to the thieves?"

"Impossible to say," said Chase. "Though judging from what the director told us, the exhibit had only opened ten minutes before it was hit, so not many visitors were inside." He tucked the baggie away. "We'll let the lab figure it out, but hopefully it will yield a clue as to the identity of these perps. If it does belong to one of the robbers, he won't be a happy camper right now. These gizmos aren't cheap."

"With the money they stole he'll be able to afford a new one," said Odelia.

"Good job, Harriet," said Chase.

Harriet beamed all over her face at this.

She was the hero of the hour! Exactly how she had dreamed it would be. But now that it had finally happened, the feeling was even better than she had anticipated.

"Okay, let's get out of here," said Chase. "And drop these off at the lab."

They said goodbye to Pinkie and told her that they'd do everything in their power to find the men who did this to her and her human, and Harriet was happy to see that the small Papillon dog was feeling better already.

"Thank you so much," she said. "I really believe that you will catch these people and return the items that were stolen to the museum."

"Have faith," said Dooley seriously as he placed a paw on the dog's shoulder. "Max is the greatest pet detective that has ever lived. If he says we will catch these people, we will catch these people. Isn't that so, Max?"

"Well..." said Max, who had never been very good at tooting his own horn. But when he saw that Pinkie's smile faltered, he made an effort to reassure her. "Of course we will find the perpetrators," he said. "Absolutely."

"I have faith in you, Max," said Pinkie, and actually placed a kiss on the big cat's cheek. Max blushed underneath his fur, and it made them all smile. For a great detective, Max was surprisingly timid when it came to associating with the female of the species.

In the car, Max gave them a short overview of the interview they had conducted with the director of the museum, and Harriet was surprised to learn that there were actually people out there who collected Nazi art.

"I don't think I would like to have a picture painted by Adolf Hitler on my wall," said Fifi determinedly.

"Me neither," said Rufus. "And I don't think Ted or Marcie would like it either."

"Apparently, a lot of the so-called Nazi art is actually fake," said Max. "So it's hard to know what's real and what's a forgery. But suffice it to say, it's definitely a lead we should follow. Oh, and the director also said he could vouch for Harold. So he's off the hook for now."

Harriet couldn't imagine that Odelia or Chase would ever

have suspected Pinkie's human of being involved, but then police people followed a different logic than the rest of the world. Harriet's gut told her that Harold was innocent, but Odelia and Chase needed more than a gut feeling or intuition. They needed solid evidence. Like the butt and the bud. She certainly hoped that Harold wasn't a smoker, and that the butt was not his. Or that he was hard of hearing. But if he was, she was sure that Pinkie would have told them. Unless she had kept information from them, of course. She wouldn't be the first pet who lied to shield her human from suspicion. But she didn't think so. Pinkie was such a sweetheart. She didn't have a scheming bone in her body, she was sure of it.

"So what now?" she asked.

"Now we pay a visit to Kurt in the hospital," said Odelia, "while Chase drops off the evidence at the lab."

Two investigations in one day. They sure had their work cut out for them, Harriet thought. But since they were all ace detectives, they could handle it—no question!

CHAPTER 14

Harold Hudspith was worried. About the heist, of course, but even more about Pinkie. Ever since he had rescued the doggie from a terrible fate by saving her life in that forest on a winter night, he had been crazy about the little thing. So to see her now so sad and downcast broke his heart. And the problem was that even though he knew exactly why she was feeling this way, he didn't know what to do about it.

After the police had conducted their interviews and had talked to him extensively, Director Stamper had sent them all home. The museum was closed for now, pending further investigation, and so there was nothing they could do there. Harold had expressed his fervent wish that the museum would open again soon, and Mr. Stamper had assured him that he would do everything in his power to make sure that the museum didn't go under. It was obvious to anyone with a brain that it would be very hard to overcome this calamity that had hit them. Even if the insurance paid out, that wouldn't do much to remedy the hit their reputation had sustained. What collector would loan them their pieces going forward? What museum would trust them to collaborate with them? And without pieces to put on display, they were doomed.

And so it was a sad Harold Hudspith who arrived home that afternoon, carrying Pinkie in his arms. But if he was sad, Pinkie was even worse. She was downright in the dumps. He gave her her favorite food, but she wouldn't touch it. He threw her favorite ball, but she didn't even give it a glance. He even took her for a walk to her favorite dog park, located on the other side of town, but she wouldn't even leave the car. And when he picked her up and carried her over to the nearby bench, she simply rolled into a ball and wouldn't engage with any of the other doggies.

When he arrived home, he was at the end of his tether. And then he got it. He'd seen something online about a famous pet whisperer who was in town at the moment for a dog show. Maybe if he paid him a visit? Perhaps he could tell him what to do? And so he searched the man's name and information online. Lonnie Love had made his fortune with several television shows that showcased his unique talent as a dog whisperer and had become the go-to person for people whose dogs displayed difficult behavior. The fact that he was in town was a real godsend because he had moved to Switzerland and had lived there for the last couple of years. He ran a dog training center where people came from all over the world. But since Harold didn't have the kind of money to send Pinkie all the way to Switzerland to be treated by Mr. Love, he would have to catch the guy now, before he left again after the dog show where he was a jury member.

It wasn't hard to find out where he was staying, as Hampton Cove doesn't have that many hotels. There was the Star Hotel on Main Street, of course, but also the Hampton Springs Hotel, near the beach. Several people had posted selfies taken with Lonnie Love and his loyal mutt Raxo, so it was probably a safe bet that's where he was staying.

And so Harold bundled Pinkie up in his arms and put her on the passenger seat of his car. She didn't even seem remotely excited to go out, the way she usually was, which told him that emergency measures were in order.

He drove them over to the Hampton Springs Hotel and arrived there in due course, parked his car, and took Pinkie up to the reception desk. The receptionist gave them an engaged smile, but when he asked if he could talk to Mr. Lonnie Love, was reluctant to give them any indication whether the dog whisperer was staying with them or not.

"It's Pinkie, you see," he explained, holding up the little doggie. "She's not herself. The museum where I work was robbed this morning, and the thieves took off with a big chunk of our collection. I think Pinkie is worried I will lose my job. She's very sensitive."

The receptionist seemed interested in the story. "I heard about that," he said. "Hitler's paintings, right? And you were there, you say?"

"I was held at gunpoint while they smashed up all the display cases," he said.

"My God," said the receptionist, a young man with a ponytail. "I'm so sorry that happened to you, sir." He glanced at Pinkie, and the doggie gave him a sad look, then her head stole out from between Harold's arms and she gave the receptionist's hand a lick. The guy practically had tears in his eyes. Then he leaned forward and whispered, "Don't tell anyone I told you, but Mr. Love is staying in the presidential suite. Though he can usually be found in the swimming pool. He loves to swim. He and Raxo both."

"Thanks, my friend," said Harold warmly.

It was indeed as the receptionist had said: the famous dog whisperer was stretched out on a pool lounger while Raxo was stretched out on his own personal lounger. For a moment Harold didn't know how to proceed. It wasn't his habit to approach famous people and harass them for a selfie or hit them with a lot of questions or personal requests. In fact, whenever a celebrity paid a visit to the museum he made sure to respect their privacy. Some of them even hired out the entire museum for an exclusive night, and even then he didn't try and chat them up. But this was different. This was Pinkie's life and health that was on the line. For her he would have done anything, and so he pulled himself together, gathered all his courage, and took the sun lounger next to the man.

"Excuse me, Mr. Love?" he asked timidly.

The celebrity dog whisperer glanced over. "No selfies," he said lazily. "If you want an autographed picture, you'll have to ask my assistant. The information is on my website."

"I'm not interested in a selfie," he said. "It's Pinkie. She's my dog, and she hasn't been feeling well. So I was wondering—"

The man held up his hand. "I'm on vacation, buddy, so I'm not taking on clients at the moment. If you want to consult with me about your dog, make an appointment."

"Yes, but Pinkie is traumatized, I think. You see, my museum was robbed this morning, and my entire wing was cleaned out by a gang of robbers. She was there and we were both held at gunpoint by the robbers. And she hasn't been the same since."

This seemed to interest the dog whisperer, as he had expected. Lonnie Love even took off his sunglasses to take a closer look at Harold and Pinkie. "Is this Pinkie?" he asked.

"Yes, this is her. She's a rescue. I saved her after her owners left her and her brothers and sisters behind in the forest on a winter night. She would have frozen to death if I hadn't come upon her, quite by accident. We've been inseparable since."

Mr. Love chewed on the temple tip of his sunglasses for a moment. "She's probably traumatized, as you say," he said, becoming more animated. "She's very sensitive?"

"Oh, yes, and very attached to me. She can probably sense I've taken this heist hard. I might lose my job, you see, if the museum is forced to close because of what happened."

"What was stolen?" asked the dog whisperer.

"The exhibit was called Art of the Third Reich," said Harold. "Mainly it was art made by members of the Nazi party. There were three paintings in the collection that were painted by Adolf Hitler himself. They were the most expensive pieces of the exhibit."

"And everything was taken?"

"Everything. They didn't leave a single thing behind. Looks like the hit was well-planned and professionally executed. These guys weren't fooling around, Mr. Love."

"Terrible," the dog whisperer murmured. "Absolutely terrible." He took Pinkie over from Harold, and much to the latter's surprise, she didn't stir. Mostly she didn't like to be handled by anyone apart from himself, so the fact that she would accept to be picked up by Mr. Love was surprising. "So you were threatened by a man with a gun, were you?" said the guy as he gently stroked the little doggie's head. "And you had to watch how they stole all of that stuff from your human. And now you're afraid he might lose his job. But he's a very good security guard, you know. And even if the museum is forced to close, I'm sure he will find another job very soon. A good man always finds a position. Isn't that so, Harold? Can I call you Harold?"

"Of course," he said.

"Look, you don't have to worry about Harold," said Mr. Love as he kept stroking Pinkie's head with his index finger and talking to her in that deep, reassuring voice of his. There was something hypnotic about it, Harold felt, and even he felt himself relax. "Harold will be just fine, and he will keep on taking care of you and you will both be A-okay. So you see, Pinkie? There's absolutely nothing to worry about. Those bad men didn't hurt Harold, and they didn't hurt you. And you will never see them again."

Pinkie gazed up at the whisperer with a sort of surprised look in her eyes, and then actually produced a sigh and placed her head on his hand and gave it a lick, just like she had done with the receptionist.

"She seems to like you," he said.

Mr. Love smiled. "I seem to have that effect on dogs. I don't know why or how, but it's always been like that. Same with Raxo over here. He was wild, you know. His owners didn't know what to do with him. He had even bitten one of them on the ankle, so they were at the end of their rope. But I took one look at him and knew I could work with him. And so I gradually earned his trust. In the end, I liked his company so much I asked his owners if I could buy him from them. They said yes and the rest is history." As he talked in his low, reassuring tone, he kept stroking Pinkie's head with gentle strokes of his finger. The doggie seemed completely relaxed in the man's arms. And when he finally handed her back, he said, "I think she will be fine. It's like you said, she's very sensitive, and after the events of this morning at the museum, she's scared and worried about what's going to happen now. But give it time and she will settle down."

"Thank you so much, Mr. Love," he said.

"Please call me Lonnie."

"What do I owe you?" he asked.

"No charge," he said as he waved a hand. "But can you do me one favor?"

"Of course. Anything," he said, feeling extremely grateful for what the man had done for him and Pinkie.

"Will you keep me informed of her progress? I'm actually curious to know how she will react."

"Of course." And so he took out his phone and they exchanged WhatsApp messages.

When he finally took off, Pinkie was resting comfortably in his arms, and he had a feeling that she would be all right.

* * *

LONNIE WATCHED the dog parent walk off and picked up his phone. Moments later, he was in touch with his supplier. "Listen," he said. "I've just been informed about the heist this morning. Lots of Nazi art being stolen? Some fine paintings by the führer?"

"Were you now?" said his contact.

"I want it all," he said. "Even if you already have other buyers lined up, I want everything. The whole lot."

"It's going to cost you."

"I don't care what it costs. I want everything, do you understand me?"

"I thought you might," said the guy. "So I've set up a private viewing at a friend's house. Are you free tomorrow? By then I will probably have the pendant, too."

"I don't need a private viewing. I said I'll take everything, sight unseen."

"I'm afraid that's not how this works," said the seller, much to Lonnie's exasperation. "You're not the only person who has expressed an interest. So either you will be at the private viewing, or you're out of the running, buddy. Is *that* understood?"

He realized that he had overplayed his hand and piped down. "Okay, fine. Just text me the time and place and I'll be there." After he hung up, he tapped the phone against his chin. He just *had* to have those pieces—he simply *had* to have them, whatever the cost. He should have known that his contact would play this dirty trick on him. Then again, it was understandable. He knew there were plenty of other collectors interested, who would be willing to pay through the nose for a chance to add these pieces to their collection. He'd just have to play it smart. Too bad he hadn't known sooner, or he could have organized something himself, though that was probably way out of his league. He might be a collector, but he wasn't a crook, even though he dealt with crooks.

But then to amass the kind of collection he had, he had no other choice.

CHAPTER 15

We arrived at the hospital to check up on our neighbor but found that we weren't the only ones who'd had this bright idea. When we arrived in the room where he was laid up, Gran and Scarlett were sitting by his bedside, both holding up a gift of grapes.

"Why do sick people always get grapes, Max?" asked Dooley.

"I don't know, Dooley," I confessed.

"Maybe grapes have healing properties that we aren't aware of?"

"It's possible," I admitted.

"Maybe *we* should eat some grapes," he said. "Even though I don't like them very much, if they have secret healing properties, we should definitely get in on that. It's not fair that humans get to keep them all for themselves and we get nothing."

"Absolutely right," said Brutus, and so he jumped up on the bedside table of the stricken man and helped himself to a grape or two. He made a face. "It tastes horrible!" he announced. "Absolutely terrible!"

I could have told him that cats aren't big fans of grapes, but it looked like he had allowed himself to get carried away.

Fifi had jumped up onto the bed the moment we arrived, and a grateful Kurt held her in his arms. "You shouldn't have," he said. "Gilda would have taken care of her in my absence."

"She was adamant to pay you a visit," said Odelia, but didn't tell the man that Fifi had been instrumental in trying to catch his shooter.

"So how are you?" asked Chase.

"The doctors tell me I will live," he said. "But I've lost a great deal of blood, so I'll have to stay here a couple of days while they try to patch me up."

"The shooter missed a vital part of his anatomy," said Gran. "Isn't that right, Kurt?"

"Yeah, a millimeter to the left or to the right and I would have been a goner," said the retired music teacher, who looked very pale, I thought. But then losing a large portion of one's blood has that effect on a person. I've been told humans get their nice roseate glow from the blood that flows through their veins. No blood, no glow, and it showed in Kurt.

The door reopened again and Kurt's girlfriend Gilda walked in. She seemed surprised to see all of us, but not unpleasantly so. She was carrying a vase and had filled it with flowers, possibly gifted by other visitors to the man.

"I still don't understand what got into the fella, though," said Kurt. "I mean, I was minding my own business, and suddenly he shot me! Just like that!"

"What do you remember, exactly?" asked Chase, whose visit didn't merely have a social and neighborly character but also an official one.

"Well, I was walking Fifi and had followed her to that old shack. You know, where all those mice and rats are." He made a face. "They should tear down that eyesore and turn the field into a nice park or something like that."

"We've all been saying that for years, Kurt," said Gilda. "But does the mayor do something about it? No, she does not," she answered her own question. "And in the meantime, we have to live with that horrible disgrace. The guy who shot Kurt was probably a drug dealer. That place is full of drug addicts lately, did you know that?"

"Since we live right next door to the field, we do know that," Chase said.

"So why don't you do something about it? Before people get killed?" She pointed to Kurt. "What will it take before you people finally get your act together? Or did Kurt have to die before you understand that things have gone too far?"

"She's very upset, Max," said Dooley.

"Understandably so," I said.

"I would be upset if my human was shot," said Rufus. "Though knowing Ted, he would never venture out into that field. Marcie wouldn't let him, especially when it's dark out. That's when the bad people come, she always tells him."

"It's all my fault," said Fifi. "If I hadn't run into that field, this wouldn't have happened." She clutched at her head. "What did I do?"

"You couldn't have known that there was a killer on the loose," I said.

"No, but Gilda has been telling Kurt to stay away from that field, but did I listen?"

"It's not your fault," I stressed. The last thing we needed was another dog with traumatic issues, like Pinkie.

"Look, there isn't a lot I can tell you," said Kurt. "I saw the guy, and before I could even ask him what he was doing there, he simply shot me."

"What did he look like?" asked Chase as he took out his little notebook.

"He was dressed in black," said Kurt as he directed a look at the ceiling. "Um… black pants, hoodie. I didn't get a good look at his face. Couldn't even tell you the color of his eyes."

"But you know for sure it was a man?"

"That's the impression I got, yeah. Though it could have been a woman."

"Anything else you remember?"

"Um…" He thought for a moment. "This probably isn't important, but just before I saw the guy, I found a red sweater hanging from a tree."

"A red sweater?"

"That's right. There was a necklace tucked into a pocket of the sweater. A gold cross. It had markings on them, but they were too small to read without my reading glasses. I figured I'd drop it off with you so you could put it in the lost-and-found."

"There was no red sweater found at the scene," said Chase as he exchanged a look with Odelia. The latter shook her head. "And no gold necklace either."

"I'm just telling you what I saw. There's probably no connection to what happened."

"All the same," said Chase. "It's good that you mentioned this."

"Yeah, that sweater could have belonged to the shooter," said Odelia.

"Look," said Gran. "Let's address the elephant in the room, all right?"

"What elephant?" asked Dooley as he glanced around.

"I think it's time that you came clean, Kurt," she said.

"Came clean? About what?" asked the man.

"About the drugs! Don't pretend you don't know what I'm talking about. It's not a crime to be a drug addict, Kurt. The problem is when you refuse to admit that you have a habit that you can't kick. And there are remedies for that, you know. Francis Reilly runs a support group for addicts, so I suggest that you sign up. You don't even have to talk during your first meeting. Simply introduce yourself and tell the good people in the group that you're an addict. In fact, you might as well go ahead and do it now."

The man was staring at Gran as if she had suddenly sprouted a second head or a third eye or something. "What the heck are you talking about, Vesta Muffin?"

"I'm talking about your habit, Kurt," she said. "It's one thing to abuse your body by using drugs, but another to bring this filth into our neighborhood. If people like you would stop using, these drug dealers would have no business coming to Blake's Field to spread their filthy poison. So just say no, Kurt. For all of our sakes. Just say no!"

"Are you suggesting that I'm a drug addict?"

"I'm not suggesting anything. I'm telling you to stop. I know it's hard, but all it takes is a little courage and some of that backbone that you've been missing all this time."

The man was gradually getting worked up, which was probably not a good idea since he had just been shot in the chest and almost killed. "Look," he said, pushing himself up straighter in his hospital bed, "I'm not going to lie here and be insulted. There's the door. Don't let it hit you on the way out! And take those stupid grapes of yours with you. Feed them to the dogs, for all I care. But not my dog," he hastened to add.

"I'm sorry you see it that way," said Gran as she raised her chin mulishly. "Scarlett, let's go. We know when we're not wanted."

"I have never taken drugs in my entire life!" Kurt yelled.

"Says you."

"It's true!"

"Then why were you shot by your own dealer? Because

you couldn't pay off your debt. And why is that? Because you've been hoovering the stuff like a vacuum cleaner!"

"I'm not an addict!"

"Oh, Kurt. Stop fooling yourself. It's not doing you any favors, you know."

"Vesta, please don't go throwing around wild accusations," Chase suggested.

"Kurt doesn't take drugs," said Gilda, also getting a little worked up, I saw. "If he did, I would know, since I practically live with the man."

"That can only mean one thing," said Gran as she wagged a finger at the woman. "That you are also a drug addict, Gilda!"

"Take that back," she hissed as she went face to face with Gran. "Take back those hateful words right now!"

"Make me!" Gran snapped.

Chase decided that it was time to fulfill one of the main roles of a police officer: that of peacekeeper. And so he positioned himself between the two women. "Vesta, I think it's time you went home. Gilda, better take a walk around the block to cool off, all right?"

"I'm not going anywhere," said Gran, in contradiction to her decision not to stay where she wasn't wanted. "You're both going to kick this habit—I want to hear you say it!"

"Your behavior is extremely insulting," said Gilda.

"I'll say," said Kurt.

"Vesta, maybe we should..." Scarlett began.

"No, I want to hear them say it!" said Gran.

"Say what?!" Gilda cried.

"That you will stop using drugs!"

Gilda and Kurt exchanged a glance, and then Gilda shared a look with Odelia, who nodded. Gilda rolled her eyes. "I will never use drugs again—not that I have ever used them before, mind you. There. Happy now?"

"Now you, Kurt. And say it like you mean it!"

But Kurt clamped his lips together, his eyes shooting twin bolts of fire at the old lady.

"Fine," said Gran. "That tells me all I need to know. Let's go, Scarlett."

And with these words, she stomped from the room, Scarlett in her wake.

"Gran is right, Max," said Dooley. "Drugs are bad for you, aren't they?"

"That, they certainly are," I said. "But if Kurt says he doesn't use drugs, I think it's safe to say it's true."

"Unless he's lying," said Harriet. "Drug users lie all the time to hide their habit, don't they?"

Fifi's eyes narrowed. "If Kurt says he doesn't use drugs, he doesn't use drugs, all right? And I should know, since I also live with the man, just like Gilda."

"That's true," Brutus admitted. "I'm sorry, Fifi. I guess you're absolutely right."

Which meant that Gran was wrong. But then why had this man tried to kill our neighbor? We still weren't any closer to the truth. All we knew was that Kurt was lucky to be alive, and Fifi was lucky to still have her human.

CHAPTER 16

A meeting had been arranged in Uncle Alec's office, but unfortunately, the chief had elected not to invite the pets to the meeting. He probably felt that four cats and two dogs were too much, and so only Odelia and Chase had been chosen to attend. The upshot was that the rest of us were all relegated to being bystanders, so to speak, and decided to pay a visit to Kingman, always a fount of information and excellent grub.

The grub situation was a little disappointing, as Kingman had managed to empty all of his bowls by himself by the time we got to the General Store, and his human hadn't yet seen fit to provide a refill. So we had to go empty-stomached for a little while longer, until we returned home, which I planned to do forthwith.

I was feeling sidelined, to tell you the truth. Not invited to an important meeting. Not being provided with any food. It was enough to put me in a bad mood. And I felt that if I wasn't going to be involved in the investigation anymore, I wasn't going to take an interest in the developments either.

And so instead we decided to shoot the breeze with our

friend and let Odelia and Chase handle things from now on. After all, they were the police investigators, not us.

"I don't think it's fair that we weren't invited to take part in the investigation anymore," said Fifi. "I really wanted to help out Pinkie, you know. She didn't look well. And also, I want to find out who did this to Kurt."

"I'm sure Odelia and Chase have it covered," I said. "Clearly they don't need our assistance, or they would have insisted we join them for this important meeting."

"I guess we'll just have to run a parallel investigation," said Brutus.

We all stared at him. "What do you mean, a parallel investigation?" asked Rufus.

"Well, you know, in tandem with the humans' investigation, us pets will run our own investigation. And never the twain shall meet," he concluded with a grin.

"I still don't get it," said Fifi. "How can we run our own investigation? We're not detectives. We don't have access to the kind of resources that Odelia and Chase have."

"No, but we have our own way of doing things. In a sense, cats and dogs are the perfect detectives since we can insert ourselves into any place unseen and unheard, and spy on our humans. And also, we can talk to other pets, and nowadays practically every house is infested with pets, so we've got our own small army of informers."

"You mean like Sherlock Holmes and his Baker Street Boys," said Rufus, and we all looked up in surprise that the big sheepdog would know about this. "Hey, I watch TV too, you know," he said. "And Ted is a big Sherlock Holmes fan. He'll watch anything about the famous detective, so I know a thing or two about investigative work."

It certainly gave me food for thought. It was true that it wouldn't be fair to leave both Pinkie and Fifi in the lurch, simply because Uncle Alec didn't want us to be present in his office for his meetings, and seemed to resent us taking part in his investigations. So maybe we should ignore our humans altogether and conduct our own investigation for a change? Make sure that we discovered who was behind the attack on Kurt and the big heist at the museum? Together we could pull it off—I was sure about it.

"Okay, so why don't we all work together on this?" I suggested. "Between the six of us we should be able to come up with a plan, wouldn't you say?"

All I saw were excited faces smiling back at me, so it looked as if Brutus's idea of a parallel investigation was a go.

"What about me?" asked Kingman. "Can't I join your investigation also? I mean, I know a lot of people, you know, and a lot of pets, of course. So I should be able to contribute to your investigation."

We assured him that of course he was welcome to participate in whatever capacity he saw fit. And so a coalition of the willing was formed: we would all put our best paw forward to ensure that justice was done, for Fifi and Pinkie. After all, pets have rights too.

"I think we should probably join forces with Gran," said Dooley. "She is the leader of the neighborhood watch, and she was almost attacked herself last night, by that strange man with the knife."

"Do you think it was the same man who attacked Kurt this morning?" asked Fifi.

"It's possible," said Dooley. "Though this man had a knife, not a gun, and killers always like to use the same weapon. Isn't that true, Max?"

"Mostly they stick to the same MO," I admitted. "But not always."

"Gran seems to think Kurt was attacked because of a drug deal gone wrong," Harriet said. "So what do we think about that?"

"Kurt is not a drug addict," said Fifi adamantly. "Gran's theory is completely bogus."

"Good to know," I said. "But if it wasn't a drug dealer that attacked Kurt, who was that man? And what was he doing in Blake's Field at that early hour of the morning?"

"He smelled like bleach," said Fifi. "And the men at the museum also smelled like bleach, so that's our first important clue: we have to find people who smell like bleach."

It certainly seemed like a very important clue we needed to follow, and one I was sure our humans would totally ignore.

"There's also the cigarette butt I found," said Harriet. "And the earbud."

"Too bad we don't have access to the crime scene report anymore," I said. "Uncle Alec will have it in his possession and he won't want to share its results with us."

"We don't need no stinkin' crime scene report," said Brutus. "All we have to do is find a man who dresses in black, smells like bleach, shot Kurt this morning, robbed a museum later on, wears a hearing aid, and smokes cigarettes." He held up his paws. "I mean, how many men who answer to that description can there possibly be, right?"

"Right," I said, though I could have told him that a lot of what he had said could simply be circumstantial evidence. The cigarette butt could have belonged to any museum visitor. The hearing aid could have fallen from another visitor's ear, and the fact that the killer smelled like bleach could be because he had accidentally stepped in it.

"I say we go home," Brutus suggested. "And talk to Gran. We could suggest to form a coalition with the neighborhood watch and thresh this thing out together. She and Scarlett have access to certain resources that are off-limits to us, and we have a wide network of pets that we can tap into to find the information we need. What do you say?"

"I say that sounds like a wonderful idea," said Fifi, and held up her paw.

The rest of us did the same, and soon we were all shaking paws on our new plan. Now if only Gran was prepared to play ball, we were in business!

CHAPTER 17

We arrived just in time to catch Gran leave through the front door, lugging a big suitcase and looking furious.

"Gran?" asked Dooley. "What's going on?"

"I'm leaving," she said. "Can you believe they've actually gone and installed a gate? As if I'm a toddler! Pretty soon they'll also put guard rails on the bed, or maybe tie me up at night! No, I've had it with these people, so I'm out of here."

"But where are you going?"

"I'm going to stay with Dick Bernstein for a while, until I decide what to do. He's been so kind to offer me a bed for the night. I could have shacked up with Scarlett, but we didn't think that was such a good idea. We get along so well these days that we don't want to ruin a beautiful friendship."

"But what am *I* going to do?" asked Dooley. He was close to tears, I saw, now that his human was leaving home.

She smiled and crouched down to tickle him under his chin. "You could come with me, if you like," she said. "In fact, you could all come with me. I'm sure Dick won't mind, and it would only be for a couple of days, until I figure out my next steps."

"Will you be living by yourself again?" I asked. "Like you did before you moved in with Marge and Tex?"

"I suppose so," said Gran. "I haven't really thought about it. But that sure sounds like a good idea. I'll have my freedom again, you know, without these two busybodies," she added as she directed an angry look at the house.

"Where are Tex and Marge?" asked Harriet.

"At work," she said. "I discovered the gate when I arrived home just now. They've gone and installed it just like they said, the idiots." She rose to her feet again. "So are you guys coming or not? No pressure," she added.

We all shared a look. It was hard to know how to proceed. "I'll be staying with Gran for sure," said Dooley. "She's my human. I can't leave her to go and live by herself."

"Then I'll also come," I said, since I didn't want to leave my friend alone.

"If you guys are leaving, I'll also join you," said Harriet. "What about you, pookie?"

"Well, obviously I'll come too," said Brutus.

"I don't think I'll join you," said Fifi. "I can't leave Gilda alone at a difficult time like this. And also, Kurt will hopefully be home soon, and I want to be here when he is."

"I better stay here too," said Rufus. "Dogs running away from home is not a good look. Ted and Marcie are liable to call the cops and start a manhunt. Or a dog hunt."

"That's fine," I said. "You both have to be with your humans right now, the same way we have to be with ours."

"But what about Odelia and Chase?" asked Fifi.

"And Marge and Tex?" asked Rufus.

"Odelia and Chase should have insisted with Odelia's uncle that we got access to the investigation," I said.

"And Marge and Tex shouldn't have installed that gate," said Dooley. "They should know better than to harass an old lady like Gran, who has done so much for them."

And so it was decided: Gran would leave home to go and stay with her good friend Dick, and the four of us would join her.

Looked like a big change was in order, and a big change it most definitely would be!

"I don't think I've ever run away from home before," said Dooley as we rode in the backseat of Gran's little red Peugeot.

"We're not actually running away from home," I said. "We're simply keeping Gran company as *she* runs away from home."

"I think it's very brave of her," said Harriet. "To go and live by herself at her age."

"If this is what she feels is best for her, she should definitely go for it," said Brutus.

"I just hope this won't interfere too much with our investigation," I said. Already our gang of six had been reduced to four, but that shouldn't be a problem. We had carried off investigations before, and with Gran by our side we should be able to make a difference.

"I hope Odelia and Chase won't be too sad," said Dooley.

"They'll live," I said, perhaps a little harsher than I had intended.

Harriet picked up on it. "Are you upset with Odelia, Max?"

"A little bit," I confessed. "She should have fought harder for us and she didn't. Which tells me that she doesn't think our contribution matters very much."

"I think she does think it matters," said Harriet. "But she doesn't want to upset her uncle either. He's not a big fan of cats participating in his investigations."

"Well, he should be a big fan," I said. "If not for us, he wouldn't have the clearance rate he has right now."

We had arrived at the home of Dick Bernstein, and I was surprised to find that it was a pretty fancy house where the man lived.

"My God," said Harriet. "Is Dick a millionaire, Gran?"

Gran smiled. "I don't think he is. But he does seem to have done well for himself, doesn't he?"

"What did he do for a living before he retired?" asked Brutus.

"Among other things he was a postman," said Gran. "But his son is an investment banker, so maybe he paid for this place."

We all got out and walked up to the front door, which opened the moment we arrived. Dick stood there, arms wide, a big smile on his face as he showed a set of perfectly white teeth. "Vesta!" he said warmly. "Welcome to Casa Dick! My home is your home, and you're welcome to stay as long as you like—what's that!" he added as he caught sight of the four of us. "Cats!" He took a step in our direction. "Shoo!" he yelled. "Get away, you filthy animals! Pssssssst!"

"Hey, those are mine!" said Gran. "Take 'em or leave 'em!"

Dick stared at her in dismay. "But they're cats! You know I don't condone cats, Vesta. They're, they're... they're messy!"

"Nonsense," she said as she stalked into the house. "They're the cleanest creatures in the world. And a darn sight cleaner than some humans I know."

The four of us followed her in, and the look on our host's face was something to behold: a mixture of surprise, horror, and regret. But it was too late now. He had indeed invited Gran into his home, so he couldn't back out.

"Keep them with you at all times, will you?" he said as he hurried after Gran. "I mean, don't let them roam around please? That hair gets everywhere, in every nook and cranny, and I'll never get it out again! It'll be on my clothes, on my carpets…"

"This is a lovely place you got here, Dick," said Gran.

He glanced around. "Yeah, it's not too shabby."

The ceiling was the same wainscoting as the walls, and frankly, I didn't like it. It seemed like a relic of the seventies, but then I've never been a big fan of putting wood on the walls and ceilings. A big fire hazard in my personal opinion. Plus, wood smells funny. But since beggars can't be choosers, I decided to make myself at home there.

"I hope he's got plenty of food for us," said Dooley as he headed for the kitchen.

"Hey, where is he going!" Dick cried.

"Looking for food, no doubt," said Gran.

"What do cats even eat?" asked Dick as he brought a pair of distraught hands to his thick white mane.

"Kibble is fine," said Gran. "So where do I sleep?"

"Um, upstairs," said Dick as he stared after us nervously. "Do they shed a lot? Maybe we should shave them?"

"There will be no shaving of my cats," said Gran. "And to answer your question: they do shed a lot, but only if you don't brush them on a regular basis, which, as it happens, I'm in the habit of doing. So don't worry, Dick. I'll take good care of them and make sure they don't get in your… hair." She laughed at her little joke, and Dick grimaced unhappily.

The kitchen was as opulent as the rest of the place, but of kibble or any other type of cat food, there was no trace.

"No cats," said Dooley sadly. "Dick doesn't have cats, you guys."

"No, I understood that," I said. "He seems to dislike us intensely."

"He probably likes dogs," said Brutus. "Often people who hate cats love dogs."

"Not Dick," said Dooley as he sniffed at the furniture. "This place has never seen a dog or a cat in its life."

It looked as if we had arrived in the home of one of those human beings who dislikes cats and dogs both. It sure was going to be an interesting and novel experience.

CHAPTER 18

Another minor point of criticism we would have put to Dick was that his home didn't have a pet flap, so we had no way to come and go as we pleased—unless, of course, he left the back door open or a window. It certainly was a far cry from what we were used to, but since this was Gran, and we wanted to support her in her struggle with her daughter and son-in-law, we were prepared to slum it for a little while.

"Let's go exploring," I said, therefore. And so we decided to split up and investigate our new surroundings, just to make sure there were no surprises. Dooley and I headed out into the backyard since Dick had conveniently left the kitchen window open, and we found that it was certainly a backyard we could approve of, with a nice hedge that closed it off from any nosy neighbors so Gran could do some sunbathing in the nude if she wanted to. There was a trampoline and some fitness gear that told us that he was a man who liked to keep himself in tiptop shape. But as a self-confessed ladies' man, he probably had to, as a lot of ladies like a man who's in shape. Gran certainly does, though I very much doubted she had any romantic notions attached to this stay at Dick's.

"Do you think Gran is in love with Dick, Max?" asked Dooley.

"I very much doubt it," I said. "Gran isn't the kind of person to fall for any man. She's too hard-nosed for that."

He laughed. "I didn't know Gran had a hard nose. It seems pretty soft to me."

I smiled. "I think life hasn't always been kind to Gran, and especially the men in her life, and so she has become a little cynical about the male species, and that includes the likes of Dick Bernstein."

There was a knocking sound, and when we looked up, we saw that Harriet and Brutus were knocking on one of the upstairs windows and waving at us. Behind them, the horrified face of Dick appeared, and he quickly took them down from the windowsill.

"He will learn to love us," said Dooley.

"I have my doubts," I returned.

We decided to enter the house again and go in search of Gran so she could feed us. All this traipsing around had made me pretty famished.

We found her in one of the upstairs bedrooms, where she was bouncing up and down on the bed, testing the mattress. "Pretty solid," she determined. "Just like at a five-star hotel. I think I'm going to like it here. And the most important thing," she said as she held up her finger, "no guard rails and no gate at the top of the stairs!"

"So where are we going to sleep?" I asked.

"You can sleep here," she said, pointing to the foot of the bed. "Or on Dick's bed, of course, if you prefer," she added with a mischievous glint in her eye.

"There's no food," said Dooley.

"And no pet flap," I added.

"Look, I know it's not perfect," said Gran, "but for now, it's the best I can do. Things will get better, I promise."

"Where do we go from here?" I asked.

"Oh, I don't know. Maybe I will move in with Scarlett after all. I mean, our friendship has stood the test of time, so it will probably withstand the two of us shacking up together. Even though we're both set in our ways, we will have to find a way to get along. But then I've always been a flexible person, so that shouldn't be a problem. In fact, of all the people I know, I'm probably the easiest person to get along with."

"Okay, so we have a proposition for you, Gran," I said.

Harriet and Brutus had also entered the room.

"Yes, we would like you to join our investigation," said Harriet.

"What investigation would this be?" asked Gran.

"Why, the investigation into the shooting of Kurt Mayfield, of course," said Harriet.

"And the investigation into the museum heist," I added.

"The lives and happiness of two of our friends hang in the balance," said Dooley. "Fifi and Pinkie."

And so we proceeded to tell her all about the new friend we had made in Pinkie and how sad she was over the fate that had befallen her human.

Gran nodded. "Okay, I will help you. Of course I will help you. Especially now that you tell me that that stubborn son of mine has excluded you from the investigation."

"We will crack this case ourselves, won't we, Gran?" asked Dooley.

"Absolutely," said Gran. "That's a promise, Dooley."

"What's a promise?" asked Dick as he walked in.

"Oh, I was just talking to myself," she said quickly. "I've promised myself that I won't be bullied anymore."

Dick smiled. "I can't imagine anyone bullying you, Vesta. You wouldn't stand for it."

"Well, my daughter and her husband have succeeded in doing exactly that," she said, "by treating me like I'm some crazy old person who doesn't know what she's doing."

"I don't see you as a crazy old person," he assured her. "In fact, I think you're probably one of the most gorgeous girls I know, Vesta Muffin."

"Cut the crap, Dick," she said with a wave of the hand. "It won't work on me."

"I know," he said with a sigh. "But you can't blame a fella for trying."

"You once told me about some connections in the underworld you had, from the days you worked as a croupier at a Las Vegas casino," she reminded him.

"Oh, you remembered that, did you?" he said. "Yeah, my boss back then was this major crime figure. Real bad news."

"So you remember Rock mentioning the museum heist this morning?"

"Sure. Lots of Nazi art stolen. Bad business."

"The thing is that the museum guard is a friend, and now he's a suspect in the investigation."

"That's too bad," said Dick.

"So I was thinking that maybe you could put out some feelers? Find out who was behind the heist? That way we could get my friend off the hook. His reputation restored, you know." She gave him her best smile. "I'd owe you."

He grinned. "Vesta Muffin who owes me. Now that would be a first." He turned serious. "I'll definitely put my ear to the ground. I still know a couple of people from back in the day. I'll ask them if they've heard anything about this heist of yours."

"I appreciate it, Dick," she said. Then hopped off the bed. "Now I've got two more requests for you: my cats are hungry, so you need to get your act together and feed them. And also: cats need a pet flap. They need to be able to come and go as they please." When he started to protest, she held up her hand. "That's non-negotiable, Dick. Pet flap and pet food—and be quick about it, there's a good boy. And now if you don't mind I'll freshen up a little and have a lie-down. I have a feeling it's going to be a long night."

"Oh, you're going out tonight, are you?"

"Neighborhood watch, Dick."

"I'll ride with you if you like," he said, a hopeful gleam in his eye.

She shrugged. "Suit yourself. But watch patrol is not for the faint of heart. Prepare yourself for a tough gig."

The retired postman rubbed his hands. "I can't wait," he said. But when Gran had disappeared into the bathroom to freshen up, his smile was quickly wiped from his lips as he regarded us sternly. Suddenly he spirited a knife from behind his back. It was of the big butcher's variety, perfect for boning a chicken—or a cat! "You," he said, pointing that knife at us. "I want you hairy rats out of here in five seconds, is that understood? And if you ever set foot in my house again, I'll feed you to the hogs. Five... four..."

And since he looked as if he meant business, we decided that it was in our best interests to do as he said.

And so within half an hour of entering our new home, we had already left it again. Suffice it to say, Dick Bernstein will probably never be our best friend!

CHAPTER 19

When Vesta left the bathroom fifteen minutes later, she was surprised to find her cats gone. When she asked Dick, he said he hadn't seen them since he had opened the door for them. "They were meowing up a storm, so I figured I'd let them out. They haven't been back."

"They're probably exploring the neighborhood," she said. "They love exploring. It's what they do."

"Are you sure about that pet flap, Vesta?" he asked. "It's going to put me back a pretty penny as I would have to install an entire new back door."

"Oh, it's fine for now," she said. That shower had been pretty wonderful and she was feeling in a mellow mood. "Just make sure they've got plenty of food and they will be happy as clams. Cats are very easy. As long as you feed them well, they're okay."

"Good to know," said Dick with a smile. "So what time do you want to have dinner? It's just that I've got a couple of friends coming over tonight."

"Oh, poker night, huh?"

"Something like that. I'd totally forgotten about it, so I'm afraid I won't be much use to you for neighborhood watch patrol tonight. But tomorrow night I'm all yours, honey."

"That's fine, Dick," she said. "Maybe I'll also stay in tonight. After all, a girl needs her beauty sleep, and the doctor…" She was suddenly reminded of her son-in-law, and since that memory carried a bad vibe, she decided not to go there. "Anyway, being out all night every night simply isn't healthy, so Scarlett and I have decided to scale back on this watch business a little from now on. After all, as my son likes to say, patrolling the streets and making sure they're safe is the work of the police, not citizens like ourselves."

"Now you're talking," said Dick. "Well, you're welcome to stay, of course. Though I'm not sure poker is your thing."

"Oh, no, it isn't. But I'll just stay in my room if that's all right with you."

"Absolutely," he said. "You have a nice night in and relax. And tomorrow maybe we can do something together. Go to the beach maybe, or do a vineyard tour. Or we could take a boat tour. One of my friends owns a pretty neat yacht. It's moored in the marina."

"No yachts, please, Dick." She remembered the last time he had invited her and Scarlett on a yacht and the engine had stalled, and they had to be towed back to shore. "But that vineyard sounds pretty neat. I love a nice glass of Beaujolais."

"You're on," he said, well pleased.

"Can I ask Scarlett to tag along?"

"Sure! Absolutely! The more the merrier. And I'll invite Rock as well, shall I?"

She had a feeling Dick was eager to pamper her and Scarlett, and she didn't mind. It was a nice change of pace to be pampered. At home, she was always having to walk on eggshells, but staying at Dick's place she felt as if she was on vacation. Taking an extended vacation in her own town. Now that was the life, wasn't it?

PURRFECT HEIST

Dick's phone chimed, and he picked up. She tripped down the stairs to check what the man had stocked in the fridge. Maybe she could start dinner prep early and return the favor to Dick for putting her up at his place by making him a nice dinner for two. Being the gourmet that he was, she was sure he would appreciate that. As she was sniffing around in the fridge, trying to decide what she could make, she heard snippets of her friend's phone conversation.

"Don't bring that stuff into my house, German. I won't stand for it. You can do what you like, but don't bring it here, you hear? I won't have it in my house."

She wondered what that was all about but didn't pay any attention to the rest of the conversation since it was none of her business. She found a plate of cold cuts and wondered if she could use it to prepare an oven dish. She wished now that she could call her daughter and ask her opinion. But because she wasn't talking to Marge after the outrageous behavior she had displayed, that wasn't an option. And so instead, she called Scarlett and told her friend all about the trip to the vineyard Dick had suggested.

"Count me in," said Scarlett. "So, how is it going with Dick?"

"Pretty darn great so far," she said. "He's got a nice place."

"Oh, you hadn't seen it yet?"

"I hadn't. You?"

"He once invited me over for dinner."

"I should have known."

"It wasn't like that. He wanted to ask my opinion on something connected to his hair."

"His hair!"

"Yeah, Dick's always been proud he still has a full head of hair, so when he started going bald he was extremely worried, so he asked me if I knew a remedy. And since he didn't want any of his friends to find out, he insisted on my absolute discretion."

"And what did you advise?"

"A hair transplant seemed like the best option in his case. And since I happened to know a great hair transplant person, I got him an appointment."

"So Dick had a hair transplant? You never said."

"He swore me to secrecy. But it's been fifteen years, so I don't think he cares anymore who knows. Especially since you can't really see the difference. They did a great job."

"It's true," she said as she studied the man, who had walked into the living room, still talking into his phone. "He looks great. And to think he once advised Tex to rub mayonnaise on his head as a remedy against going bald."

"That was very mean of Dick, wasn't it?" Scarlett laughed.

"Not mean enough," she said.

"Oh, honey. You should make up with your family. It doesn't do to fall out like this over a trivial thing like that gate they installed. The only reason they did it is to make sure you don't fall down the stairs and break your neck. It means they care about you, that's all."

"I don't care why they did it. They shouldn't have done it. Treating me like a baby—like a prisoner in my own home. Anyway, if things don't work here at the house, can I come and stay with you?"

"Of course. Though it's going to feel a little cramped after staying with Dick."

"That's all right," said Vesta. "We'll make it work." Even though Dick was being very nice to her, she had a feeling she wouldn't enjoy staying with him for more than a couple of days. And since the last thing she wanted was to go home, she could already foresee her and Scarlett living together for the foreseeable future. "Wouldn't it be nice to live together?"

she said. "I think we'd have a lot of fun. We could have a pajama party."

"Absolutely," said Scarlett, though she didn't sound completely convinced. Vesta thought the biggest problem was the cats. Scarlett and her living together in a small apartment was fine, but add four cats and things might get a little cramped. But then maybe the cats could stay home, and they could visit them as much as they liked.

She'd miss them, of course. It wouldn't be like now when they lived with her. But that couldn't be helped.

She hung up and rubbed her hands. "I'll cook us a nice dinner, shall I?"

Dick grinned. "Oh, Vesta, I'm going to enjoy this so much!"

CHAPTER 20

Since it was obvious that we weren't welcome at Dick's place, we decided to return home. When Gran found us gone, she would probably call her daughter, and the latter would tell her all about Dick's scandalous behavior and make sure that she knew what kind of person she was staying with. However, when we finally did arrive home, it was clear that all communication between Gran and the rest of the family had been severed.

"She hasn't called, and she won't pick up her phone!" Marge cried the moment we entered the house.

"She's staying at Dick Bernstein's place," Harriet said.

"But Dick has kicked us out," said Brutus.

"He doesn't like cats," I explained.

"He's not a very nice man," Dooley added.

"Dick Bernstein! What is she doing there!" Marge cried. She seemed overwrought, and I was starting to appreciate that Gran leaving home was probably a bigger issue than I had thought. Clearly, the fact that she had left home had caused a sort of panic.

"I told you that she would be fine," said Tex. He stood

behind his wife and had placed his hands on her shoulders in a reassuring gesture. "She needs a little time to cool off, that's all. She'll be back before you know it." The smile on his face told us that he didn't seem to mind that his mother-in-law had left home as much as his wife did.

"You should never have installed that gate," said Marge.

"I didn't want her to fall down the stairs and break her neck," said Tex. He sighed a sort of wistful sigh, and the look on his face clearly belied his words. If it had been up to him, he wouldn't have installed any gate at all, so the idea must have come from Marge. "And I didn't even get started on those bed rails yet."

"That would have been the last straw. We probably would never see her again."

"She'll be back," said Tex sadly. "I can't imagine she will be staying with Dick permanently. And besides, he wouldn't like it either."

"She wants to go and stay with Scarlett," said Harriet.

"Scarlett lives in an apartment," said Marge as she bit her lip. "Imagine if she starts sleepwalking there. She's liable to fall out of a window."

"Imagine that," said Tex wistfully.

"We have to tell Odelia. She can go and talk to her and convince her to return home," said Marge. "She won't listen to us, of course. She considers us the enemy now."

"After all that we did for her," said Tex, shaking his head.

Marge glanced at me. "Max, maybe you can talk some sense into her? Or you, Dooley? I know she listens to you guys."

"We've been kicked out of Dick's house," I reminded her. "He threatened us with a knife and said that if we ever set foot in his house again, he will feed us to the dogs."

"I think he said hogs," Brutus corrected me.

"Dogs or hogs, it's not a fate I would enjoy."

"He had a very big knife," said Dooley, and shivered at the recollection. "And it looked like he meant business."

"Okay, this is just too much," said Marge, throwing up her hands in despair. "What a day this has been! Kurt is shot, and my mother decides to run away from home to shack up with a notorious womanizer who threatens to kill our cats and feed them to the dogs!"

"The hogs," Brutus murmured.

"Whatever!"

"It'll be fine," Tex assured her, patting her shoulders.

She shook off his hands. "This is all your fault!" she cried as she turned on him.

"My fault?"

"If only you hadn't installed that gate!"

"If only," said Tex. Judging from the smile fixed on his face, he seemed to have a recurring dream of his mother-in-law lying at the foot of the stairs with a broken neck.

"I'm calling Odelia. She has to fix this. And if Ma doesn't want to come willingly, Chase will simply have to arrest her and handcuff her to the bed if that's what it takes."

"You can't drag your mother home against her will, Marge," said Tex. "If she doesn't want to live with us anymore, that's her prerogative."

Marge deflated a little. "Yeah, I guess you're right. She's a grown woman, and she can do what she wants." She released a sigh. "Okay, fine. Maybe we'll just have to accept that things will be different from now on. Very different."

That was certainly an understatement.

"So now that Dick has kicked us out," said Dooley, "how are we going to conduct our investigation, Max? Gran won't be able to help us, will she? And Odelia doesn't need our help or want our help, so it's just the four of us from now on."

"I guess if that's the way it's going to be," I said, "that's the way it's going to be."

And since I was still upset with Odelia, I decided that for the present, I wasn't going home either but would stay at Marge and Tex's place. And so I settled down on the couch. The first thing a good detective does is use his little gray cells after all, and what better way to use those little cells than to let them rest and come up with fresh ideas? And so after I had eaten my fill, I hunkered down on the couch and promptly fell asleep.

I woke up from loud noises coming from the kitchen. I recognized them as Odelia and Chase, engaged in a discussion with Marge and Tex.

"What do you mean, Gran has run away from home?" Odelia was saying.

"She didn't like the little gate I installed at the top of the stairs," said Tex. "Even though I only put it there to prevent her from breaking her neck."

"I think you did the right thing, Dad," said Chase.

"I know I did the right thing," said Tex. "But Vesta doesn't seem to agree."

"Where is she?" asked Odelia.

"She's staying with Dick Bernstein at the moment," said Marge. "And she's thinking about moving in with Scarlett."

"This is a disaster," said Odelia.

"She'll be fine," said Tex.

"Maybe it's for the best," said Chase. "If she doesn't like it here anymore, a change of pace will do her good. Right, Dad?"

"Absolutely," said Tex. "A change of pace is always good."

Marge and Odelia didn't seem to agree, but it was out of their hands—and our paws. And so I closed my eyes again, and only opened them again when I became aware of someone sitting on the couch next to me and placing their hand on me. When I looked up, I saw that it was Odelia, and so I immediately slipped out of her grasp and tripped out of the living room.

"Max?" she asked, much surprised. "What's wrong?"

But since I didn't feel I owed her an explanation, I snuck out through the pet flap and was soon entering Ted and Marcie's backyard, where I was sure she wouldn't follow me.

Rufus was happy to see me. "Hey, buddy. I thought you were going to stay at Dick Bernstein's place?"

"He kicked us out," I said. "Can I stay with you for a while?"

"You haven't run away from home also, have you?"

"Something like that," I admitted.

"But why? You have the best humans known to man."

"Odelia feels she doesn't need us anymore for her investigation. And I feel insulted."

"I'm sure she didn't mean it like that," said Rufus.

But since I was convinced that she did mean it like that, I wasn't going to be convinced by my canine friend's specious arguments. And so I stretched out next to him, and soon was dreaming of delicious kibble and maybe a juicy pork chop. I know it's probably not good for me, but I love it all the same.

CHAPTER 21

Night had fallen when I woke up again, and I stretched out luxuriously. Time to head out to cat choir and talk to some of my friends and get their opinion on what was going on in Hampton Cove. My flight from the house had caused me to lose sight of Dooley, Harriet, and Brutus, but I was sure I'd see them at the park. And so I set out on my own, walking the sidewalk in the direction of the park. I was feeling a little weird, without Gran and my human and also without my friends, but then life sometimes throws you these curveballs, doesn't it? I'd just have to try and deal with them as best I could.

On my way to the park, I wondered if maybe I shouldn't make a detour and check up on Gran. Dick may have kicked us out, but that didn't mean I couldn't sneak back in and see if he was treating Gran with the respect she deserved. And also, if she was still in the habit of sleepwalking, she might need some assistance from a helpful cat like me.

It wasn't long before I arrived at the street where Dick lives, and as I snuck into the backyard and glanced in through the window, I saw that a meeting of some kind was taking place in there. Several white-haired men of Dick and Gran's age sat gathered around the living room table playing a game of cards. Scarlett was also there, and so was Rock Horowitz. The table was laden with bottles of wine and the atmosphere was festive. People were laughing, and Gran appeared to be having a ball with her friends.

I felt a little sad. She seemed to have forgotten all about us already, and was settling into her new life with these people very easily, as if we had never existed at all.

Given the events of the day, this wasn't conducive to me feeling on top of the world—quite the contrary. And so I slunk off again, feeling that Gran didn't need us anymore.

When I arrived on the sidewalk, I almost bumped into Dooley. He stared at me. "Max!" he said. 'We've been looking for you!"

"I was staying at Rufus's place," I said.

"I wanted to look in on Gran," he said.

"I just did. She's having a great old time."

"She is?" He looked disappointed. "I thought maybe she would be missing us, you know."

"She clearly isn't missing any of us," I said.

He didn't seem to believe me, so together we returned to the house to look in on his human. When he saw how much fun she was having, he was as disappointed as I was.

"You were right, Max," he said. "Gran doesn't need us anymore. She has moved on."

"I'm sorry, buddy."

"She's probably right. She has been staying with us for so long she must be sick and tired of having to look at our faces every day. Change of scenery, you know. It happens."

"Where are Brutus and Harriet?"

"Cat choir," he said curtly. And so we commenced the long trek to the park. "I don't understand, Max. I thought Gran loved me, you know. And now she doesn't even seem to care what happens to us. Dick kicked us out of the house and she doesn't even care."

"Maybe she doesn't know he kicked us out," I said.

"But Marge must have told her, right?"

"She's not talking to Marge, or to any member of our family."

"Too bad," he said. "Someone should tell her that she's staying with a cat hater."

She probably wouldn't care if she had turned a new leaf and had left her old life behind. We were part of her past now, and she was looking into the future.

"You have to sort things out with Odelia, Max. She was very worried about you, you know."

"She doesn't need me anymore, buddy, and that's all there is to it," I said.

"But she does need you. She told me so herself. Wanted to know what you thought of this whole business with Kurt and also the heist. I said you were still looking into things."

"I'm sure she was simply being polite," I said. "Clearly she has also turned over a new leaf and will be conducting her investigations without us from now on." And maybe she was right. After all, who in their right mind enlists their cats in their investigations? Probably no one. And so I was more convinced now than ever that we should confine ourselves to doing what most cats did: eat, sleep, and be merry. This police business wasn't our business.

We arrived at the park in due course, and set a paw for the playground, where the jungle gym, the swing and the seesaw were already occupied by dozens of our friends, who were shooting the breeze and generally happy to enjoy one another's company. I knew I wouldn't be very good company, so I stayed on the sidelines as much as possible, with Dooley being the one who engaged our friends in conversation.

Even though I was no longer a pet detective, I still felt a little sad. Which was odd, since cats shouldn't do their humans' work. It goes against the nature of who we are.

And I would have sat there for the rest of the evening if not a familiar-looking dog sidled up to me and gave me a nudge. "And?" she asked. "What have you found out, Max?"

It was Pinkie, and I wondered how she had found me.

"I'm afraid I don't have a lot of information for you yet, Pinkie," I said.

"That's all right, Max. I know you're working hard, and these things take time. I did some sniffing around myself, you know, and I've come to the conclusion that the thieves must have cased the museum."

"They did?" I asked.

"Why else did they arrive so early in the morning, just after opening time? They must have picked the moment with the least number of visitors. And also, they made a beeline for the room with the Nazi art, so they must have known exactly where to find it."

I smiled. "Cased the museum. You're already familiar with the vernacular."

"Like I said, I've been investigating on my own. I cannot do nothing, Max. It's too important for Harold."

"No, you're right," I said, and suddenly felt guilty that I had been so wrapped up in my own dramas that I had neglected to honor the promise I had made to Pinkie. "Look, I haven't given your case my full attention yet," I said. "But I will, I promise."

"The thing is, Max, that if they cased the place in advance, there must be CCTV footage, right? And since it would have stood out if they had been wearing masks, they will be on camera with their faces unhidden. So maybe you could ask your humans to check the CCTV footage of the days and weeks leading up to the heist. Maybe something will jump out at them. Men behaving suspiciously or something like that, you know."

I would have told her that I was no longer talking to my human, but that wouldn't have sat well with Pinkie, so I didn't. Instead, I promised I would do whatever I could to find the men who had done this to Harold, and to return the items that were stolen to the museum as soon as possible.

I didn't know how I would go about it, especially since I was essentially working solo now, but I owed it to her to at least give it my best shot.

And since my friends were all having such a great time, I decided to sneak off and start my investigation. After all, there was no time like the present.

CHAPTER 22

My first port of call was the museum. I didn't know what I hoped to find there, but was hoping for at least something that would inspire me as to my next steps. The place was locked down for the night—maybe indefinitely after what happened that day, and I only stayed there for a couple of minutes before I decided that it wasn't going to do me a lot of good to hang around there the entire night. The crooks had probably escaped in a getaway car, but the police would have checked that out—possibly followed them using CCTV and street cameras. But if that had led to something, I hadn't been informed. No arrest had been made yet, so probably the crooks had used a stolen vehicle and fake plates, which wouldn't have given the police a lot to go on.

Next stop was the field where Kurt had been attacked. For some reason, I was convinced that the two cases were connected somehow. Call it a hunch, but that whole bleach business kept me wondering about a possible link. The shack where I ended up was deserted at that time of night, as it should have been, especially now that Gran was staying with Dick and couldn't go sleepwalking there for the time being.

Possibly she was sleepwalking in Dick's neighborhood right now. I sat on the bench where Gran had sat the night before, and pondered how to proceed. Mostly, inspiration simply comes to me, and as I glanced up at the full moon rising over the horizon, suddenly I thought I heard a sound. It seemed to be coming from a nearby bush, and when I hopped down from the bench and snuck over, I saw that several people were hiding in those bushes. For some reason, they were all dressed in black and wearing masks.

Odd, I felt. There wasn't anything of interest in those bushes or in the field in general. Unless they were there to catch rabbits. They could be poachers, looking to snag a free meal, and it was true that the field is full of rabbits. But for some reason, they didn't strike me as poachers. And also, their attention seemed to be riveted on the houses that overlook the field. One of the men was looking through a pair of binoculars, whispering things like, "I think the coast is clear, young guns. I think they've gone to bed."

"And even if they haven't gone to bed," said one of his colleagues. "We're still going in there, aren't we?"

"I'd much prefer to do this the easy way than the hard way," said another.

"Or we could simply ring the bell and ask them to hand it over," said a final voice. The voice sounded familiar. And when I looked a little closer, I thought I recognized... Gran!

Now what was she doing here, staking out our neighbors? It didn't seem like an activity of the watch, and besides, none of these people were members of the watch.

And since I'm essentially a very curious kitty, I snuck up to her. When I gave her a nudge, she seemed startled.

"Gran," I whispered, "what is going on?"

"Shhh," she said quietly.

"Who are these people?" I asked.

"Shhhhhh!" she repeated, clearly not in a chatty mood.

"Okay, let's go," said what must have been the leader of the small group.

"Ouch, my arthritis is acting up again," said one of the people present, and it was only now that I realized that this was none other than Dick Bernstein!

"Oh, don't fret, Dick," said the man next to him. "With me it's my knees. The doc says they're shot to hell."

If I wasn't mistaken, this was Rock Horowitz!

Now what the heck was going on here?

The leader of the gang moved off, and the others followed. Behind me, another person came hurrying up. "Wait for me!" she cried, and I recognized her as Scarlett Canyon! So was this a mission of the watch or not? Whatever it was, I was determined to get to the bottom of it, and so I followed the five-man crew to wherever they were going.

"Max, you stay out of this," Gran hissed when she saw that I was following along.

"Only if you tell me what's going on," I returned.

She stubbornly refused to enlighten me, and so I tracked their movements, hoping it would tell me what their plan was. Catch a thief? Rumble a group of dealers? With the neighborhood watch, you never know what might go down, which is part of its appeal.

We had reached the backyards that line the field on this side, and with some effort, they all clambered over a fence and dropped down into a backyard that didn't look all that dissimilar from our own. It belonged to a couple named Morris and Lindsey Elford, who had probably lived there even longer than the Pooles. I saw them around the neighborhood from time to time, and also at block parties, where Lindsey's potstickers were always popular and so was Morris's sangria—though not with us cats, of course.

It took quite some effort to climb that fence, since at least the four members of this team I knew were all septuagenarians, and the leader was probably not a whole lot younger. In other words: a gang of elderly watch members making themselves useful by fighting crime in our neighborhood. I thought it was all very noble, and I supported their efforts wholeheartedly. Until the leader took out a bag of tools and started fumbling around with the lock on the back door of the house whose backyard we had entered.

Was he... breaking in? Now that seemed incongruent with the goals and objectives of the neighborhood watch. Then again, maybe they were simply trying to ascertain whether someone else had already broken in and wanted to catch this person in the act.

But as we snuck into the house, I saw that the place was completely dark, and of a burglar, there was not a single trace. It was then that I realized that the burglars... were us!

"Gran!" I hissed. "What are you doing!"

"Keep quiet!" she returned, unhappy that I had trailed them all the way there.

I followed them up the stairs, and when the leader started rummaging around in what looked like a study, I realized he was looking for something very specific. I didn't know what it was until he had found it.

"Got it!" he whispered as he held up what looked like a pendant of some kind. "The idiots kept it in a drawer!"

Just then, the lights went on in the corridor, and I heard footsteps. "Who's there?" a voice asked.

"Get out of here!" the leader cried, and suddenly there was a sort of feverish activity when the five watch members —or burglars—scrambled to get away.

A man had appeared in the door and was holding what looked like a shotgun in his hands. He was wearing a red and black dressing gown and didn't look happy to see us.

"Stop right there!" he said, and aimed his shotgun in our general direction!

The five-man team didn't pause to take in the view, but instead, they hurried down the stairs, then out of the house and along the backyard. And as we were running for the fence, suddenly a gunshot rang out in the night. There was a sharp cry, and Dick yelled, "I've been shot! I've been shot!"

He still managed to crawl over the fence, assisted by the others, and moments later, we were all running for cover and didn't stop until we had reached the old shack.

The members of the small group all stood panting heavily, with Dick yelping in pain. "He shot me," he said quietly so as not to draw attention. "That idiot shot me!"

"Where did he get you?" asked the leader of the gang.

"My leg," said Dick.

They had all taken off their masks, and I saw now that the leader was one of the men I had seen playing cards with Gran earlier that evening. He didn't look familiar, but he must be a friend of Dick's, for he seemed very concerned when he examined his friend's wound. "It's just a flesh wound," he finally determined. "You should be fine, buddy."

"I don't feel fine," said Dick. "It hurts."

"Flesh wounds always do," said the guy curtly. He now took out the trinket they had stolen and examined it. "It's the real deal," he said with satisfaction. "Amazing quality."

"How much will it fetch you?" asked Gran.

"A hundred thousand at least," said the guy.

Scarlett whistled through her teeth, something I didn't even know she could do. "Nice chunk of change, German."

"I might get even more," said German. "I've got several buyers on the line. One of whom is very eager to get his hands on this little thing. I might even be able to drive the price up to a cool million. But only if I play my cards right." He gave them all an appreciative look. "You did good tonight," he said. "I wasn't convinced when Dick told me that he could vouch for you, but I can see now that he was right and I was wrong."

"So what's next?" asked Gran.

"I've got another little job tomorrow night, if you're interested. Not as tricky as this one, mind you. A small-time collector in town. He's rumored to have a couple of pieces that are worth taking a closer look at. And contrary to this couple, he won't be home."

"I hope not," said Dick. "I don't want to get shot two nights in a row!"

"Let's get you to a hospital, shall we," said Gran.

"No hospital," said German. "Too many questions."

"Then what? We can't leave Dick like this," said Scarlett.

"We won't," said German. "Better come back to my place, and I'll patch you up."

Dick groaned. "You're not a doctor, German."

"No, but I used to be a vet. Same difference." Dick was shaking his head, and the guy got a little annoyed. "It's either that or you might as well turn yourself in. Your choice."

"All right, let's do it," said Dick finally. "But next time we better make sure nobody's home."

"I didn't have a choice in the matter," said the guy as he assisted Dick to hobble off in the direction of the road. "We needed to hit the target now. My main buyer will be out of the country next week, so it was either now or not at all."

"Fine, let's just get out of here," said Dick.

Gran and Scarlett stayed behind the others as they started their return journey.

"Tell me what's going on, Gran!" I insisted. "Or do you want me to tell Odelia what you've been up to?"

"I'm undercover," she whispered back. "Isn't it cool?"

"Undercover? You've just robbed these people!"

"I know! All par for the course for the watch!"

"You better tell Uncle Alec," I said.

"Not yet," she said. "First, I want to know how high this thing goes—or how deep—and catch all the members of the gang!"

I finally thought I understood. "Is this… are these the people that hit the museum this morning?"

"That's right. Can you believe my good fortune! The person I'm staying with is best buddies with the actual leader of the Gray Panthers!"

And with these mysterious words, she hurried off after the others. I watched them all get into a van and drive off, and wondered what Gran had gotten involved with now.

It certainly wasn't the kind of thing that gave me the warm fuzzies!

CHAPTER 23

In spite of the way Odelia had snubbed me earlier that day, I felt this was too important not to bring to her attention. And so I decided to return home so I could place her in possession of the facts posthaste. It felt a little awkward to be sneaking into my own home and up the stairs, but then matters had progressed too far for the misgivings I was experiencing to stop me from doing what I felt was right.

I entered the bedroom and jumped up onto the bed to find... that my human wasn't there! And when I looked over, I saw that Chase wasn't there either! And when I finally checked Grace's bed, I saw that she was also absent.

Now where could they all have gone? And since I'm not the kind of cat who likes to twiddle his thumbs, I hurried next door to look for Marge. Oddly enough, the same scene played out there, with the couple's bed not having been slept in.

As I stood in the backyard, I wondered where all of my humans had gotten off to. And so I saw no other recourse but to ask Rufus, our usually well-informed neighbor.

The big sheepdog was resting peacefully in his doghouse as he often does on warm nights and didn't even seem surprised to see me again. "I've kept a space for you, buddy," he said, as he moved over. "Just settle in for the night and tomorrow I'll show you where I keep my best kibble."

"Thanks, Rufus," I said. "But you wouldn't by any chance know where my humans have gotten off to, would you?"

He gave me a strange look. "But I thought you weren't on speaking terms with them anymore? Something about an investigation they didn't want you to be a part of?"

"I know, but I just saw Gran break into the house of a neighbor, and so I need to tell them about that."

"She's a burglar now? Are you sure? She doesn't seem the type."

I didn't know that you had to be a certain type to be a burglar, but since I didn't have the time to argue, I simply said, "Have you seen them, yes or no?"

"Um, I think I saw them all leave in a hurry. They all got into Chase's squad car and took off around... oh, maybe eleven o'clock or something."

"Where did they go, do you know?"

"No idea," he said. "They didn't stop to tell me, and they didn't tell Ted and Marcie either. But then I guess your humans have always been very attached to their privacy. They don't like to share their plans with their neighbors. And nor should they, you know. I mean, it's one thing to be on good terms with your neighbors and another to—"

"Thanks, Rufus," I said, interrupting his flow of words. "I'll see if I can't find them."

And off I was, leaving my host for the night looking a little disappointed. I guess when you're expecting a guest to stay the night and all of a sudden he's off like a hare, it makes your head spin. It certainly made his head spin, and it doesn't take a lot to make the big sheepdog's head spin.

I entered the house again, looking for clues about where my humans might have gone off to, but unfortunately couldn't find anything. And I was just walking out through the flap when Dooley, Harriet, and Brutus came walking in.

"Max!" said Dooley. "We've been looking for you!"

"Looks like everyone is looking for everyone tonight," I said. "I was looking for our humans. You wouldn't have seen them, would you?"

"You mean... they're gone?" asked Dooley.

I nodded. "Rufus says they left around eleven, in Chase's squad car. But he doesn't know where they went."

"I don't remember if they had some important engagement," said Harriet. "Have you checked the calendar?"

We popped back into the house to check the calendar, which is stuck to the fridge with a magnet. But as far as I could tell, there was nothing of importance for that day.

"I don't get it," said Harriet. "What's with everybody today? First Gran takes off, then you take off, Max, and now our humans take off? Must be something in the water?"

"I didn't take off," I said. "But I met Pinkie and I felt so bad that I decided to continue our investigation. And since you guys were having such a great time, I didn't want to trouble you."

"You can trouble me anytime, Max," said Dooley. "As it was, I was troubled to find that you had left without telling me."

"I'm sorry," I said. And then I told them about Gran and Dick and Rock and Scarlett and their nocturnal adventure with a man named German.

"I don't believe this," said Dooley. "Gran has turned to a life of crime now?"

"I think she has infiltrated a gang," I said. "There's a difference."

"She still broke into that house," said Harriet. "That constitutes a crime, doesn't it?"

"I'm not sure it does," I said. "I would argue that it's a gray area."

"There's nothing gray about it," said Brutus. "She's a burglar—end of."

"I like Dick even less now," said Dooley. "First, he gets rid of us, and now he introduces Gran to his gang."

"Are you sure she said this is the same gang that robbed the museum this morning?" asked Brutus.

"That's what she said," I said. "But there have to be more members, since Pinkie told us there were six gang members this morning, and I only counted three now, if I include Dick and Rock, and I'm not even sure if they were present this morning. They could also have infiltrated the gang on behalf of the neighborhood watch."

The watch is one of those organizations that enjoys a rotating lineup, not unlike some rock bands, like Deep Purple or Fleetwood Mac or Guns N' Roses. Though I had never realized that Dick and Rock were members of the watch, that didn't mean they weren't. After all, Gran is the boss, and she can invite whoever she likes to her party.

"Gran is really off the reservation," said Harriet as she shook her head. "We have to stop her, you guys, before she goes and does something really stupid."

"I don't know about you," said Brutus. "But breaking into a house and robbing her own neighbors feels pretty stupid to me. She could go to jail for this."

"Oh, no!" said Dooley. "That means I will never see her again. Unless I pay her a visit in jail. Are cats even allowed to pay a visit to prisoners in jail?"

"I'm sure they are," I reassured him. "And like I said, Gran has probably infiltrated this gang and isn't guilty of a crime at all."

"Undercover Gran," said Dooley appreciatively. "That sounds a lot better already. That means she could come out of this thing a hero and receive a medal for bravery."

"Either way," I said, "we have to find Odelia so we can tell her what Gran is up to."

If only we knew where they were. And as we sat there, thinking hard thoughts about our humans who would simply leave like this without telling us, Fifi came tripping up to us from next door. "I know where your humans are," she said.

"Where?" I asked.

"Something happened to Kurt," she said. "And they took off immediately."

"What happened to Kurt?" I asked.

She shook her head sadly. "I don't know, but it can't be good, because when I asked to tag along, they didn't take me. That means it's probably pretty bad, isn't it? Very bad?" she sniffed. "Maybe he's even… dead?"

CHAPTER 24

We arrived at the hospital and immediately set foot for the third floor, where we had last seen Fifi's human. And since she felt she needed all the emotional support she could get, she had asked her best friend Rufus to tag along. I wasn't sure how Rufus's humans would have felt about that, but since we didn't bother to ask, we would never know.

The nurses we passed all gave us strange looks, but then maybe they had never seen cats and dogs traveling in a single pack before—or possibly not in this particular setting. Hospitals are very picky about personal hygiene, and for some reason we still have this reputation that we aren't the most hygienic of pets. A reputation that is absolutely unfounded, I can tell you, since cats are extremely hygienic, and Fifi and Rufus are, too.

We arrived at the room where Kurt had been holed up that afternoon and didn't waste time bursting in through the door. Much to our elation, we saw that Kurt was still alive. Or at least he had his eyes open and seemed animated.

Around his bed, I saw that our entire family had gathered,

and also Gilda, who probably hadn't left his side since the incident that morning that almost cost him his life.

All those present seemed surprised to see us, but not unpleasantly so.

"Odelia, I have to tell you something very important," I said, straight out of the gate.

"Oh, Max," she said as she picked me up in her arms. "I'm sorry if I did something to upset you," she whispered into my ear, making sure that Kurt or Gilda didn't notice. They are amongst the majority members of the human species who can't talk to cats, you see, and wouldn't have understood that Odelia likes to share her confidences with us.

"Well, you excluded me from the investigation," I said. "And so yes, I was a little upset about that. But that's not important right now."

"I didn't exclude you," she said, sounding surprised.

"You didn't want me present at the meeting with Uncle Alec this afternoon," I reminded her.

"That wasn't me. That was my uncle acting strange again. He gets like that from time to time. Thinks that cats don't have a place in his investigations."

"So... it wasn't you who didn't want us present?"

"Of course not! I wanted you to be there, like always, but he put his foot down and said no way, José."

"Who is this José?" asked Dooley, interested. "I don't think we've met him."

"Okay, then I'm sorry for jumping to conclusions," I said. "But that's all unimportant in light of recent events." And so I told her all about the burglary I had witnessed Gran perpetrating, along with Scarlett, Dick, Rock, and a man named German.

She seemed even more shocked than I was that Gran would be involved in something so nefarious.

"She shouldn't have done that," said Odelia, and tapped

her husband's arm. They removed themselves from the room for a moment, and as they stepped out into the corridor with me, she explained to me that Kurt had suffered a sudden setback, and that the doctors had worked on him to get his heart pumping again. For a while, it had looked touch and go, but then he had finally pulled through. It had certainly given Gilda a big scare, and so they had all hurried out to the hospital to be there for their neighbors.

"I don't believe this," said Chase as Odelia told him about what Gran was up to. "Although, that's not entirely true. I do believe it. In fact, it's probably exactly the kind of thing she would be up to when left to her own devices." He raked a hand through his mane. "We have no alternative but to raid Dick's house and place them all under arrest."

"But Dick and Rock are probably working as neighborhood watch members," I told Odelia. "The real culprit is this German fella, and the rest of his gang also."

Odelia thought about this for a moment and nodded. "If we bust Dick now, we might lose a great opportunity to catch the whole gang," she told her husband. "Maybe we should simply trust Gran. She might be able to pull this off."

"Or she might get herself and the others killed," Chase grunted unhappily.

"Do we have a choice? If we arrest them now, we might never know who the other members are, and we might never see those stolen museum pieces again. Especially since the gang leader already has a buyer lined up."

"A buyer who is leaving the country next week," I reminded them.

It was a tough decision: trust Gran or not?

In the end, Chase decided to put his faith in the old lady. But only because he didn't have another choice.

I could see where he was coming from. If I were him, I would have found myself between a rock and a hard place also. Gran is not the kind of person who is easy to put your faith into. She is fickle, cantankerous, and utterly unreliable. Tough to entrust the fate of an investigation to a person like that!

"Okay, you and the others," said Odelia, "will keep an eye on Gran, is that understood? Make sure she doesn't get in way over her head."

"Dick doesn't like us," I said. "He kicked us out of the house, and he said that if we didn't leave he would cut us up into little pieces and feed us to the hogs."

"Surely you mean dogs."

"Pretty sure he said hogs."

"That's not good," Odelia agreed. "But Gran needs you right now, Max. So you go back there and do whatever you can to help her close this case, all right?"

I gulped. The prospect of being fed to the hogs didn't exactly sound appealing to me. But if Odelia thought we needed to keep an eye on Gran, she was probably right.

She hugged me close. "I'm sorry you thought I was excluding you," she said as she pecked a big kiss on the top of my head, then removed a few hairs from her lips. "You couldn't be further from the truth. I will never exclude you from my investigations, buddy. I care too much about you to do that, and I appreciate that big beautiful brain of yours too much."

"Okay, you're forgiven," I said as I tried to wrestle myself loose. All this hugging is all well and good, but there are limits to the level of affection a cat can take!

CHAPTER 25

Chase told us that he had heard about these Gray Panthers that Gran had mentioned. He had thought that perhaps they were an urban legend, but now it would appear they were all too real.

"Who are the Gray Panthers, Max?" asked Dooley.

The four of us were on our way to Dick's house to follow Odelia's instructions and make sure that Gran didn't come to any harm.

"Well, according to Chase, they are a gang of robbers that are famous for a number of high-profile heists they have carried out over the years," I said. "All of them are rumored to be of a respectable age and have been career criminals all of their lives. But they only started to gain notoriety when they formed a gang and started their string of heists that have targeted the most famous museums and private collectors and relieved them of some of their most priceless possessions. Their heists are always carried out to perfection, well-prepared, and they've never been caught. Which is why Chase said he had always believed the rumors to be just that: the figment of someone's imagination."

"And now Gran is a member of the Gray Panthers," said Dooley. "I'm so proud of her!"

"There's nothing to be proud of," said Brutus. "If these are the same people who almost killed Kurt, the only place they belong is behind bars, respectable age or not."

He was right, of course. If a member of the Gray Panthers had shot Kurt, it was imperative he was caught as soon as possible, before he shot someone else.

"Will Kurt be all right?" asked Dooley. "He didn't look so hot."

"The doctors said the worst is over, but he will take a long time to recover," I said.

"He had a narrow escape," said Brutus. "Considering he was shot at point-blank range."

"We still don't know why he was shot," I reminded them. "So best to be careful. If the shooter is a member of this gang, we might come across him at some point. And if he shot Kurt, there's no telling what he might do to us if he believes we pose a threat to him."

"I just hope he won't shoot Gran," said Dooley. "Or Scarlett. He should shoot Dick instead."

"He shouldn't shoot anyone," I corrected my friend.

"Not even Dick? But he was very mean to us."

"Not even Dick," I confirmed. "Even if he was mean to us."

"If all the people who are mean to cats deserve to be shot, there would be a lot less people on this planet," said Brutus.

"I don't believe that," said Dooley. "Everybody loves cats, surely?"

"Not everybody," said Brutus with a laugh. "Dog people, for instance. A lot of them don't like cats. And then of course there are the people who don't like dogs *or* cats. Few though they may be, there are people like that out there."

"Like Dick," said Dooley stubbornly. Clearly, the man had

made quite a bad impression on our friend, and he wasn't going to let him forget it.

We had arrived at Dick's place and walked around the back to see if we couldn't find a way in. Dick might not be a big fan of the pet flap, but that didn't mean his house was fully cat-proof. And so we managed to find an open window on the second floor, which wasn't hard to reach with the passive assistance of a convenient tree. The moment we were in, we went in search of Gran, with Dooley especially expressing a fervent wish she hadn't been shot and killed by that horrible man who had shot Kurt.

We found Gran in bed, peacefully asleep, and also Scarlett, in the next room. We also found Rock and Dick, but of the other members of the Gray Panthers, there was no trace.

"Well, at least they're alive," said Dooley, blowing out a sigh of relief. "And now we won't let them out of our sight, all right?"

"All right, Dooley," I said. "We won't let Gran out of our sight for a single moment."

And so we took up position at the foot of the old lady's bed. And I would have closed my eyes for a nice nap if Gran hadn't stirred and kicked off the blanket to get up. It was the middle of the night, so this was unusual behavior. But Dooley didn't seem to think so. "It's happening again," he said. "See? Her eyes are open but she's still fast asleep."

We followed her out of the room and into the next room, where she started rummaging around in one of the wardrobes for some reason.

"At least she's not outside trying to feed the birds," Dooley said. "She seems to think she's some kind of bird lady."

She certainly wasn't a bird lady now, as she rooted around in that wardrobe until she had found something that was hidden underneath a pile of neatly ironed white shirts that must have belonged to Dick. It was a small trinket and it looked very familiar to me. It was, in fact, the pendant that she and the other members of the Gray Panthers had stolen from our neighbors, the Elfords.

"Now, will you look at that?" said Brutus. "Gran has found something."

"It's the necklace that was stolen from Morris and Lindsey Elford," I told them. "Dick must have hidden it here."

"And Gran has found it," said Dooley. "She really is an amazing thief, isn't she? A worthy member of the Gray Panthers."

I could have told him this wasn't a good thing, but Gran was already on the move and was taking the trinket to her own room, where she proceeded to hide it under the mattress, perhaps to take out later and admire as it was a very nice and shiny bauble.

She slipped underneath the covers, a satisfied smile on her face, and promptly dozed off again—though it could be argued that she was never awake. It's hard to tell with these sleepwalkers. They seem to be awake, but apparently they're not. Very confusing!

THE NEXT MORNING we were awakened by a cry of anguish. It seemed to come from the next room, and when we hurried over, we saw that Dick stood rooting around in the same wardrobe Gran had been so interested in last night. He was throwing all of his nice shirts onto the floor, possibly in search of the trinket he picked up last night. He must have heard a noise, for he wheeled around, and when he saw us, yelled even louder.

"Hi there, Dick," I said. "Guess what. We're back!"

CHAPTER 26

Dick didn't seem overly pleased to see us, and the feeling was mutual, I have to say. "I told you to stay gone!" he hissed.

But then his screaming must have woken up Gran, for she came shuffling into the room, looking sleepy. "What's with all the racket?" she asked. Suddenly, she saw us and her eyes widened, and a wide smile lit up her face. "Oh, my sweethearts!" she cried, opening her arms wide. "Come here! Dick, my darlings are back!"

"Yes, I see," said Dick with a grimace. "Such a nice surprise."

Gran bundled us all in her arms and gave us a big hug. It certainly warmed our hearts, and Dooley gave me a wink. "We'll never let you out of our sight again, Gran," he promised her.

"That's good to hear," she murmured. She got up and clapped her hands. "Who's ready for a big breakfast? I can eat a horse!"

"You haven't seen the pendant we took last night, have you?" asked Dick as he scratched his head.

"What did you do to your shirts, Dick?" asked Gran. "Why are they on the floor?"

"It was right here," he said. "If I don't find it, German will be very upset. And you don't want to get German upset. He's not very nice when he's upset."

"We'll find it," said Gran with a careless gesture of her hand. "Let's have breakfast first. Who's coming?"

And since the four of us were pretty much starving at this point, we eagerly followed her down the stairs and into the kitchen, where she proceeded to yank open the fridge in search of something she could use to prepare breakfast.

Scarlett came tripping down the stairs five minutes later, but of the two men, there was no trace. Possibly they were looking for the bauble that Gran had hidden under her mattress. I didn't think it was prudent to tell her about that, though, since it was a stolen item and should be returned to its rightful owners posthaste.

"Gran, what's the deal with these Gray Panthers?" asked Dooley. He had jumped up onto the kitchen counter and was determined to get to the bottom of this whole strange business.

"Oh, that," said Gran. "Well, they're some kind of Robin Hoods. They steal from the rich to give to the poor. I kinda like them, I have to say. Their leader is a man named German Kilburn, and he seems to have this whole thing figured out."

"But if they're the men who robbed the museum yesterday," I said, "you can't really call them Robin Hoods, can you?"

"Yes, that heist has caused a lot of trouble for the people involved," said Harriet.

"And especially for Harold Hudspith, the museum guard," I said.

"It's all fine," said Gran. "Those museums and the collections they house are all insured to the hilt. They might even make money on this deal."

"Not Harold," I said. "He will lose his job."

"And what about Kurt?" asked Brutus. "A member of your gang shot him, Gran."

"It's not *my* gang," she said. "I've got nothing to do with them. Like I told Max last night, I infiltrated the gang to find out more about them, and while doing so, I met their leader, and he struck me as a very impressive person, I have to say. Very…" She directed a look at the ceiling for a moment. "Forceful, if you know what I mean. Energetic. And very handsome, too. Did you know that guy is sixty-eight and is still strong as an ox? And he still has all of his hair," she added. "And not because he had a hair transplant, like Dick did. Hair transplants are cheating," she added for good measure.

"Looks like you admire this man," said Dooley, confused.

"Well, in a sense I do," said Gran. "Like I said, he's like a modern-day Robin Hood, he and the other members of his gang."

"How did you get involved with them?" I asked.

"They were all here last night," said Gran. "They're friends of Dick, somehow, and they regularly meet for poker night. And so last night when we were all enjoying a nice game of cards, they said they urgently needed to get their hands on some trinket for some reason or other, but the other members of the gang all had something else going on, so German asked if we could tag along. And since I figured it couldn't hurt to see what was going on, we decided to join his gang—or I should probably say infiltrate his gang."

"You joined a gang?" asked Dooley, fully aghast.

"I *infiltrated* a gang," she corrected him. "As members of the watch, we try to take down these gangs by working from the inside. See what makes them tick, you know."

"But Gran, you're not seeing what makes them tick," said Dooley. "You *help* make them tick!"

"Yes, Gran," I said. "Breaking into a person's home and stealing their personal stuff is an offense. You could go to prison."

"Nonsense," she said. "I did what any person would do when they're confronted with an opportunity like this: I went undercover in this gang, and now I know what they're up to, I will… I will…" She hesitated. "Um, so I guess I will…"

"You will go to the police," I said helpfully. "And give them the names of all the gang members, starting with your friend Robin Hood with the nice head of hair."

"I suppose I could do that," she admitted. "Or I could infiltrate them some more. Go a little deeper. Find out what's going on, you know."

"But you know what's going on," I said. "Now you have to do the right thing and get them all arrested and make them pay for their crimes."

She sighed. "Such a nice head of hair," she said wistfully as she started whisking a couple of eggs in a bowl to make a nice omelet. "I like a full head of hair on a man. And he's so kind, you know. And intelligent. And charismatic. And handsome, of course."

I shared a look with my friends. Looked like Gran had fallen under the spell of this gang leader and was considering becoming a full-fledged member of the Gray Panthers.

This definitely was not a good thing!

CHAPTER 27

We decided to convene in the backyard to discuss the dilemma we were facing. Gran obviously wasn't going to take down this gang, if she was in love with the gang leader. And if she was proven to be in league with the man, she might be sent to prison herself if Chase and Odelia clamped down on the Gray Panthers. A difficult position to be in.

"We have to renounce her," said Harriet. "She's obviously gone down the wrong path and has become a criminal herself."

"We can't renounce Gran," said Dooley. "She's my human. I can't renounce my human."

"No, I guess you can't," said Harriet. "So *we* have to renounce her."

"But she will go to prison," said Dooley. "I can't have my human go to prison! I don't even know if cats are allowed to visit their humans in prison. Not even Max knows."

"Like I said, I'm sure it's possible," I said.

"But what if you're wrong. I might never see Gran again!" he cried. "No, we have to make sure she isn't arrested."

"She hasn't committed a crime yet," said Harriet. "Or has she?"

"She was present last night when the Gray Panthers stole that pendant from the Elfords," Brutus said. "In my book that constitutes a crime—and not a gray zone, Max," he added, remembering our conversation from last night.

"I guess so," I said. "Unless she can prove beyond a reasonable doubt that she was working for the police. And Uncle Alec will certainly testify in his mother's favor."

"Unless he sees this as a chance to put her behind bars once and for all," said Brutus cheerfully. But when Dooley gave him a sad look, he quickly amended his statement. "He won't," he assured our friend. "Uncle Alec loves his mother. He loves her dearly."

I wasn't so sure about that. More like he tolerated her. Though of course you can love a person and still not agree with everything they get up to. Plenty of criminals are in prison and still their mothers love them. Even the worst offenders.

"Okay, we have to come up with a plan," I said. "Before these Gray Panthers drag Gran deeper and deeper into their gang."

We all thought for a moment, trying to figure out what to do. And we might have come up with something if Dick hadn't stepped out of the house and closed the door behind him. He glanced over his shoulder and then crouched down next to us. "Didn't I tell you guys to get lost? Didn't I tell you I would slice you open and gut you like pigs?"

"No, you told us you would *feed* us to the pigs," I said.

"Or the dogs," said Harriet. "That part isn't entirely clear."

"Just leave, will you?" he said. "I don't like that you guys shed all over my house. I'm allergic to cats, and the mere sight of you makes me sick." He coughed. "I mean that literally," he added for our benefit. "Literally sick." He coughed again, and sneezed.

"You mean you're allergic to cats?" I asked.

"I'm allergic to cats," he said in response to my question. "And dogs. And plenty of other things. But I don't want Vesta to know. If she knew I was allergic to cats, she would probably be out of here before I could finish telling her about the fine antihistamine drugs that are on the market today that alleviate a lot of the symptoms. She doesn't like men who don't like cats, so I can never be upfront with her about that." He sighed. "I don't mind telling you I've always had a soft spot for Vesta. She's one fine lady. Feisty, tough, and pretty irresistible. But with you guys here I look like a fool, coughing and sneezing." A tear trickled down his cheek. "See? It's happening. Pretty soon I'll be a blubbering mess and she will be out of here." He was down on his knees now, and had folded his hands in a gesture of prayer. "Please leave now. I won't feed you to the dogs."

"See?" said Brutus. "I knew it was dogs, not hogs."

"I just said that to get you guys out of here." There was a noise behind us, and he moaned. "Oh, God, here she comes!" He quickly got up. "Hi there, Vesta," he said. "I was just telling your cats how wonderful it is to have them with us."

"I'm glad they came back," she said. "Life just isn't the same without a couple of cats in the house, is it?"

"No, it sure isn't," he said with a grimace. He was blinking, I saw, and it was true that his eyes had turned a little red-rimmed. Poor guy, I thought. So that's why he wanted us out of there. Not to look weak in front of the woman he loved.

"If you want you can play with them," she said. "They love it when you play with them. Especially Dooley. He's the most playful of the four. He loves a ball on a piece of string, don't you, buddy?"

And with these words, she returned inside to finish

preparing breakfast. The smells coming from inside the house were something, and my stomach was already rumbling.

"I do love a piece of string," Dooley confessed. "But I don't want to put you out, Mr. Dick."

"Let's make a deal," he suggested. "You guys leave now, and I won't tell her that you pooped in my bed last night."

"We didn't poop in your bed last night," I said.

"You didn't poop in my bed last night. But she doesn't know that. I will tell her you pooped in my bed last night and she will believe it. And then there will be hell to pay." He smiled with satisfaction. "Nobody likes a cat that poops in the bed. Not even Vesta."

"She won't believe you," I said.

"She might not believe me," he said. "Which is why I pooped in the bed myself and I've kept the sheets. That way she will *have* to believe me. It's a nice big poop, too."

"You're a disgusting human being," I said, with feeling.

"That's just nasty," said Brutus as he made a face.

"Gran will know the difference between human poop and cat poop," said Dooley confidently. "She can smell the difference."

"I'm not so sure about that," I said. "But anyway, Gran won't mind. She loves us so much she won't care one bit."

"I'll tell her right now," Dick threatened. "I'll show her the bed sheets and she will kick you out. Just wait and see."

I smiled at the guy. "Do it," I said.

"I'll do it," he said.

"Go for it, Dick."

He gave us a look of uncertainty, then returned indoors. "Vesta, those cats of yours will have to go," he announced.

"Oh, and why is that?"

"Because they pooped in my bed last night."

"Is that a fact?" She didn't seem overly concerned.

"I can show you the bed sheets," he said.

"That's fine. You don't have to show me. It's probably Dooley. He gets anxious when he can't sleep in his own bed. I should have known. Strange place, strange people—it just gets to him, the poor thing."

"But... you have to send them home," said Dick.

"Oh, don't you worry," said Gran. "He'll be all right. He can sleep with me tonight, and he'll be just fine, just you wait and see. Okay, breakfast is ready." She positioned herself at the foot of the stairs and bellowed at the top of her lungs, "Scarlett! Breakfast!"

Dick looked crestfallen. "But what about the sheets?"

"I'll wash them for you if you like," she said. "It's just poop, Dick. Nothing to get upset about. Poop doesn't stain."

The argument had been put to bed, and even though Dooley seemed slightly upset that Gran had accused him of pooping in our host's bed, at least we hadn't been kicked out. Just then, the doorbell rang, and when we walked through the house to see who it was, the man of the hour strode in. It was German Kilburn—the leader of the Gray Panthers himself. And it was as Gran had said: he was one impressive and handsome man. And he had a full head of hair.

CHAPTER 28

"Okay, so where is the item?" asked the gang leader. "My client will be here any moment to close the sale. I've already got him up to half a mil, which is pretty good. I've also decided to give him first dibs on the Kirsten Gilmartin stuff, since he's so eager."

Behind him, more members of his gang had trickled in. Apparently, this was a big moment for them, as they stood to collect a great deal of money from the sale of the items they had stolen.

"The thing is, German..." said Dick, looking extremely nervous. Combined with his red-rimmed eyes, and the fact that he was sweating profusely, he looked as if he was about to collapse.

Rock had also joined the small gathering in the living room, and while Gran was shoveling breakfast onto plates and placing them on the table, Scarlett was there to give her a helping hand.

"Where is it, Dick?" asked German, giving the man a curious look.

"Well, I hid it upstairs last night," said Dick, "but when I went to look for it this morning…"

"Breakfast is served!" Gran yelled as she took a seat at the table and took a good long whiff from her omelet. "Mm, smells delish," she said.

"What are you babbling about?" asked German, apparently not in the mood to enjoy the breakfast that Gran had prepared.

"Well, it was gone," said Dick finally, as he hung his head dejectedly.

For a moment, the gang leader didn't speak. "I don't understand," he said. "How can it be gone? It was there last night?"

"It was there last night," Dick confirmed.

"I saw it myself," said Rock, lending his good friend a helping hand. "It looked nice. Though I wouldn't have believed it was so valuable if you hadn't told me, German."

"Just tell me where it is, Dick!" said German. "Don't play games with me, all right? I'm not in the mood!"

"I put it underneath a pile of my shirts," said Dick. "But when I looked just now, it was gone. I don't know where it could be." He directed a look at me, for some reason, as if he suspected me of having taken the item.

"I didn't do it," I told him. "I don't steal stuff. I'm not a Gray Panther."

"More like a Blorange Panther," Brutus quipped.

"Max is not a thief," Dooley confirmed. "He would never take what doesn't belong to him. Contrary to you, sir, who are a thief. And also a murderer."

German fixed a pair of furious eyes on Dick, and I was actually starting to feel sorry for the guy. "Show me," he growled.

And so the gang all trudged up the stairs to go and look for the thing.

Gran, meanwhile, seemed absolutely unaffected by what was going down. "Yummy, isn't it?" she said. "Too bad the others are missing it. You should eat your omelet when it's hot and freshly made. Don't let it get cold."

"I agree," said Scarlett. "These are really good, Vesta. What's your secret?"

"No secret," said Gran. "Just a little bit of cream," she said with a smile, "and also cheese. I find that it's the cheese that gives it that special flavor, don't you?"

"What's taking them so long?" asked Scarlett, referring to the group of men upstairs.

"No idea," said Gran. "Dick seems to have misplaced something."

"Careless," said Scarlett as she pronged a piece of omelet and closed her eyes with relish as she bit down on it. "It's so fluffy. Melts in my mouth. I love it, honey."

Gran smiled. "I'm not much of a cook, but I do know how to make an omelet."

Suddenly there was a lot of commotion upstairs, and next thing we knew, Dick had dropped down to the lawn. Looked as if he'd been thrown from an upstairs window.

Gran and Scarlett immediately got up. "Dick!" Gran cried as she came to the man's assistance. "What happened?"

"Did you fall out of a window?" asked Scarlett.

Dick didn't respond. Possibly because he had sustained a nasty knock to the head.

"Watch out!" Scarlett cried. Suddenly a second person came flying out of the window. It was Rock, and he landed right next to his friend.

"It's raining men!" Dooley cried.

"What the heck?" said Gran as she shook her fist at the group of thugs upstairs. "What do you think you're playing at, you hoodlums!"

"They've stolen something that belongs to us," said the

guy who had done the throwing. He was very big and hairy and looked like a gorilla, I thought.

"That's still no reason to treat a person like this, Willie!" said Scarlett.

The man narrowed his eyes at Scarlett. "You were here last night, weren't you? You know where the pendant is?"

"I'm sure I don't know," said Scarlett, seeming to realize that maybe she shouldn't have mouthed off against the guy. Never shout at the person who likes to throw people out of upstairs windows would have been my advice.

"Get her," said German, the big charismatic gang leader.

"With pleasure, boss," said Willie, and showed us a set of crooked teeth.

"Um… maybe we should make ourselves scarce," said Scarlett.

"Yep, I think that might be solid advice," Gran agreed.

And so both ladies broke into a run. Unfortunately for them, these panthers might have been gray, but they were still panthers, and so they caught up with the two ladies in next to no time.

"Hey!" said Gran. "You can't do this to us! Let go of me, you brute!"

The two ladies had been brought back to the house and were now being interrogated by the gang leader. He was smiling and seemed to respect Gran a great deal, for he never raised his voice, contrary to the guy who had been doing the throwing.

"Okay, so I don't think I've impressed upon you how important this deal is to me," said German. "This one pendant alone will net us half a million. But only if we find it. No pendant? No money. See?"

"Oh, I see, all right," said Gran. "But I still don't appreciate you throwing our friends out of windows. That's not a nice thing to do, German."

"I know it's not a nice thing to do, but you can understand how important this bauble is to me, can't you?"

"Oh, absolutely. And if I knew where it was, I would tell you. Of course I would."

Dooley turned to me. "Do you think we should tell Gran where it is?"

"No, I don't," I said.

"But what if they throw her out of the window too?"

"Or worse, shoot her," said Brutus.

"They wouldn't shoot her, would they?" said Harriet. "They're brutes but they're not killers, surely. Oh, wait, yes they are."

"Just tell us where it is," said German, still talking in friendly tones. There was an underlying sense of menace to his demeanor, though, and it was clear this was a man who was used to getting what he wanted.

Gran smiled. "I don't know where your bauble is, German. But maybe you should ask Dick. He must know, since this is his place. He probably took it and hid it."

The gang members turned to Dick and Rock, who were still stretched out on the lawn and weren't moving. Then they turned back to the two ladies. "Tell us where it is and we won't have to use any heavy-handed techniques to make you talk," German suggested.

"But we don't *know* where it is," said Scarlett.

German sighed. "Okay, take them both upstairs," he told Willie the goon.

The other members of the gang didn't seem to agree. "I think you should take a closer look at this Dick fella," said one of them, a sprightly old man with a nice and shiny bald head. Gran probably didn't like him.

"Yeah, seems to me Dick is crooked," said a third member of the Gray Panthers.

All of them were old, I saw, but still in pretty good shape.

I would have pegged the youngest one as in his mid-sixties, and the others in their early seventies. Gray panthers was an accurate description, all of them career criminals with a long rap sheet.

Suddenly German's eye fell on me, and he grinned. Then he grabbed me by the neck. "Okay, Vesta, if you don't start talking right now, I'll wring this one's neck. And if that doesn't loosen you up, I'll wring the neck of every one of these cats until you tell me where my pendant is."

Gran's face sagged. "And here I thought you were one of the good guys," she said. A nasty gleam had come into her eyes, and she seemed to have lost that happy smile that she had displayed from the moment she had woken up that morning. Clearly, she was seeing her hero in an entirely new light—one that wasn't as favorable as it had been before.

I gulped a little. It isn't a lot of fun to dangle suspended from a person's hands.

"Talk!" the guy yelled.

"I won't," said Gran, that mulish streak in her asserting itself again. She had folded her arms across her chest and gave the man the dirtiest look she had ever awarded anyone. "But I can tell you right now that if you harm one hair on my cats' heads, you'll be sorry, buddy boy."

The other panthers all laughed. "Oh, she's feisty!" said Willie.

"She'll sing a different tune soon enough," said Baldie.

"When I get her to fly like a bird," said Willie, "she'll sing like a canary!"

Just then, the doorbell rang, and German gestured with his head. "Go and see who that is."

"What did you say, boss?" asked Baldie, putting a hand to his ear.

"I SAID: SEE WHO THAT IS!" the gang leader yelled.

"Right, boss," he said, and hurried off to open the door.

In the meantime, German put me down again, just to be on the safe side.

The man who entered looked familiar somehow, and when he saw the collected company, displayed a jovial smile. "Where's the party?" he asked.

I saw that he had brought a Rottweiler with him, which wouldn't have made Dick happy. But since he was out for the count, he wouldn't even notice that his house was now infested by the two species he disliked the most. The dog immediately focused his attention on the four of us and started licking his lips in a sort of slavering fashion.

"Cats," he said in a low growl. "Ooh, I love cats!"

And without awaiting his master's command, he made a beeline for me!

And so I did what any cat would do: I started racing around the room, this crazy dog on my tail. I scurried up the walls, up the curtains, along the breakfast table, upending the nicely laid-out crockery, and finally jumped on top of German Kilburn himself, accidentally dislodging the man's toupee and taking it down with me as I fell to the floor. He grabbed for his bald head, and Gran yelled, "Your hair! It's not even real!"

"Raxo, here!" yelled the new arrival.

But Raxo wasn't going to miss this chance to catch himself a cat, and so the chase continued unabated. Pretty soon wallpaper was peeling from the walls, curtains came crashing down, the ceiling lamp smashed to the floor, dishes and pots and pans came clattering down from the racks above the kitchen island, and several members of the Gray Panthers sustained serious injuries when I used them as climbing poles.

In the end, Dooley, Harriet, and Brutus all joined in, and the thing turned into a free-for-all. A raging tornado of fur and claws and teeth, wreaking destruction on the room and its inhabitants.

Finally, Raxo stupidly bumped into his own human, knocking him to the floor, and they both came rolling to a full stop against the hearth. The four of us had mounted the stairs and had found a perfect hiding place under Gran's bed, where we proceeded to stay for the time being.

"That is not a nice doggie, Max!" Dooley cried, as we all panted up a storm. "Not a nice doggie at all!"

"You can say that again," I said.

In the meantime, I had finally placed the newly arrived guest. If I wasn't mistaken, he was none other than Lonnie Love, the well-known dog whisperer, famous from many a TV show and also his own popular YouTube channel that catered to millions of viewers.

I wondered what he was doing there, though I probably should have known that a man who was so enamored with big and rabid dogs would turn out to be a collector of Nazi art. And as we lay there under the bed, an item dropped through the bed slats. It was the pendant German Kilburn had been looking for. It had fallen right on top of my head. And as I shook it off, it lay there on the floor, and we all stared at the thing.

"It's very pretty, isn't it, Max?" said Dooley. "Very shiny."

"Half a million," said Brutus. "This thing is worth half a million bucks!"

"Now what?" asked Harriet.

"Now we call in the cavalry," I said.

At least if that crazy dog didn't kill us first!

CHAPTER 29

"I wonder where the rest of the stuff is," said Brutus.

"What stuff?" asked Harriet.

"Well, the stuff that the Gray Panthers stole from the museum. It must be somewhere here, or they wouldn't have asked this buyer to come and get it."

It certainly was a sample of excellent deduction on Brutus's part, I thought. But even if the stuff was on the premises, there wasn't a lot we could do about it, not with Raxo roaming around and eager to turn us all into cat fricassee.

"We have to let Odelia and Chase know what's going on," I said. "And somehow make them come to the rescue."

I felt a little silly now that we had stopped Chase from making a bust as he had wanted to. Then again, he would have arrested German but not the rest of the gang, and also not the buyer.

"This buyer fella," said Harriet. "Doesn't he look familiar to you guys? Almost as if I've seen him before."

"He's a famous dog whisperer," I said. "He has a show on television and everything."

"That's why I recognized him!" said Harriet. Her face sagged. "He's not a very successful dog whisperer, though, is he? He can't even control his own dog."

"No, he seems to have absolutely no control of this Raxo at all," Brutus agreed. "Maybe this whole dog whisperer thing is just a scam?"

"His career will almost certainly be over once it becomes known that he's been buying stolen goods," I said.

The problem was that we were effectively stuck. I had a feeling Raxo was still roaming around, trying to locate us, so if we emerged from Gran's room, he would chase us down again. Tough to alert one's human when you're facing such a formidable foe.

"I have an idea," said Dooley. "One of us should attract Raxo's attention and keep him busy while the others make a break for it." He gave me a grave look. "I'll do it. Gran is my human, after all, so I'm partly to blame for this situation."

"Of course you're not to blame for this," I said. "Not even partially. The only ones who are to blame are these Gray Panthers. And the dog whisperer, of course. They're the ones who put this whole thing in motion, not you, Dooley."

"Thanks, Max. But Gran is still my human, so I feel responsible for her behavior, you know. So I feel very strongly that I should be the one to distract that vicious dog while you guys go and look for Odelia and Chase."

"Are you crazy!" said Harriet. "That monster will eat you alive!"

"No, he won't," said Dooley. "Not if I stay one step ahead of him. I could climb a tree, for instance," he suggested. "Everybody knows that dogs have a very hard time climbing trees, so he won't be able to get me. But he will stay busy while you escape."

It was certainly an idea worth pursuing, I thought, but it didn't sit right with me that Dooley would sacrifice himself like this. And so I had a better idea. "Why don't *I* try and lure Raxo away while the three of you make a break for it? And I'll do exactly as Dooley suggested: I'll climb to the top of a tree and make sure that Raxo remains on the spot."

"I don't like it," said Dooley. "I don't think you'll make it, Max. I mean, you are a very large cat whereas I am much smaller and will be up that tree a lot quicker."

"And I'll have you know that I'm very quick off the mark, and I can climb trees like no other." The only problem I seem to face is that I can never get down without the assistance of a pair of burly and intrepid firefighters. But once this gang had been collared there would be plenty of time to get me out of the tree again.

"Look, I think I should do it," said Brutus. "Odelia is your human, Max. You should be the one to tell her what's going on. It's only fair."

"And I feel that maybe I should stay behind and do this distracting business," said Harriet. "I mean, even a loathsome creature like Raxo will appreciate what a rare and unique specimen I am, and he won't harm a hair on my head—I just know he won't."

"I wouldn't be too sure about that," I said. "That dog is vicious! And not only that, he's also stupid, so he might not even take a good look at you before he digs his teeth into your hind leg and drags you down from that tree and devours you with hide and hair."

Harriet gulped at the word picture I had painted.

"No, I think I should do it," I said. "That way you can save Gran and Scarlett from these horrible people."

"I will do it," said Harriet adamantly.

"No, I will do it," said Brutus. "I feel as if it's been ages since I made myself useful in an investigation."

"I will do it," said Dooley. "It was my idea in the first place."

"Look, the longer we sit around arguing," I said, "the less of a chance Odelia and Chase will have of arresting these people. So we have to make up our minds right now, you guys."

"I will do it," said Harriet.

"No, I will do it," said Brutus.

"I will do it," said Dooley.

"I think I should do it," said Harriet.

"I insist," said Brutus.

"No, *I* insist," said Dooley.

"Ladies first," said Harriet.

Oh, dear.

In the end, fate decided for us when a dog came sniffing underneath the bed. It was Raxo, and he seemed overjoyed that he had found us. Immediately, he began barking up a storm. Unfortunately for him, he didn't fit underneath the bed, so he couldn't quite get at us. But that didn't stop us from panicking at the sight of the big dog and the sensation of spittle flying around our ears. And so the four of us ran for cover—a different cover than the one we had already been enjoying. The dog raced after us, happy as a clam that the game was on again and that he could destroy more of Dick's house in the process.

We flew down the stairs, the dog hot on our tails, and when we slammed into the living room, Lonnie Love screamed, "Raxo, no! Heel! Heel, Raxo!"

But Raxo was having too much fun chasing us to do any heeling, or whatever it was that his master wanted him to do. To the people present, we were nothing but a blur as we passed through on our way to the backyard. And when the four of us all raced up the only tree of note in Dick's haven of verdant green, and were distributed evenly amongst its branches, I realized that we had put ourselves in quite the pickle.

Raxo was barking up a storm down below, anxious to get at us, and so once again, we were stuck. Only this time was even worse than before. We had no way down from there, and that dog looked as if he was prepared to stick around for as long as was necessary.

He was motivated, he was energized, and he was excited.

In other words: he was in it for the long haul!

CHAPTER 30

Grover Hopegood was cutting his hedge when he became aware of strange goings-on at his neighbor Dick's place. First, Dick was flung out of an upstairs window, and then soon after, Dick's good friend Rock Horowitz suffered the same fate. For a moment, Grover, a retired long-haul trucker, wondered if perhaps this was a new pastime for his neighbor, who often boasted about the different hobbies he had entertained in the past, amongst which were as a kayaker conquering treacherous whitewater rivers, or climbing the highest mountains or even diving in the deepest most dangerous cave systems. Maybe he was now adding diving from windows to the list of daredevilry?

Even though some of Grover's other neighbors had once told him that none of it was true and that Dick had simply been a postman all his life, whose hobbies had never extended beyond playing a game of pool at his local pool hall, nevertheless Dick certainly had always struck him as an impressive figure. A handsome man, and very charming, as Grover's wife Martha could attest. She held a torch for Dick, something

Grover didn't quite know what to think of. Then again, he'd always felt it was important to get along with one's neighbors if one wanted to have a peaceful and quiet life, as he preferred. Ever since he had retired from driving his big rig, all he wanted was to spend as much time as he could tending to his backyard and his flowers, and apart from that, he had no other ambitions in life except to stay healthy and live as long as possible.

"Martha," he said as he stopped snipping the tips of his hedge for a moment. "You have got to see this. Dick and Rock just came flying out of an upstairs window."

Martha, who had been enjoying the pleasant rays of the sun and reading a bestseller, reluctantly closed the book and came over. An attractive woman several years Grover's junior, it still amazed him she had ever accepted his wedding proposal fifty years ago this fall, and had given him three strapping sons. "What's all this about Dick jumping out of a window?" she asked, happy for the distraction. Whereas Grover enjoyed life in the suburbs, he often got the impression that Martha found life a little too tedious for her taste. People flying out of windows was exactly what she needed to break the monotony.

"He didn't jump," said Grover. "He was thrown. By that big fellow over there."

He pointed to the big guy who stood looking out of the window and who looked like a gorilla.

"But... why does Dick want to fly out of his own window?" asked Martha uncertainly.

"Unless he didn't," said Grover, as it started to dawn on him that maybe something more nefarious was going on next door than a simple case of daredevilry.

"Maybe we should call the police," Martha suggested. "Maybe Dick is being robbed in his own home. A home invasion, you know. You read about this stuff all the time."

"Dick isn't rich, though," said Grover. "Mostly these people seem to target the rich."

"Better call it in," Martha suggested. "Dick doesn't look as if he's fully on board with this business of throwing him out windows."

She was sure right about that, Grover saw. Dick and Rock had both flown through the air just fine, but considering that they weren't getting up again, they may have broken a couple of bones when they landed, or maybe even have broken their necks.

He didn't like that. If Dick died, the house would be sold, and who knew who they would get as a new neighbor. You knew the neighbor you had, but you didn't know the neighbor you might get. And even though Dick wasn't the perfect neighbor by far—too many noisy parties in the summertime—he definitely wasn't the worst one either. The fact that he allowed Martha to use his pool from time to time was an added benefit.

And so Grover took out his phone and dialed nine-one-one. And he was just placing the phone to his ear when he saw four cats come racing out of the house being chased by possibly the largest and meanest-looking dog he had ever seen.

Moments later, those four cats had all scooted up Dick's tree and seemed determined to stay there for the time being. The dog hunkered down at the foot of the tree and shared their sentiment.

In other words: it was a good old-fashioned standoff.

"Hampton Cove Police Department," a voice spoke on the other end of the call. "What's your emergency?"

"Well, my neighbor has just been thrown out of his upstairs window," he said. "And now he's not moving anymore. His friend was also thrown from the same upstairs window and I believe they could both be dead. They sure look dead to me."

The dispatcher seemed oddly interested in this story, for she asked a couple of follow-up questions and then assured him that she would send a patrol car to come and check and also told him not to interfere.

"Oh, I have absolutely no intention whatsoever of getting involved," he assured her. "The guy who did the throwing looks like a mean son of a gun, and I don't want him to do the same thing to me that he did to Dick and Rock."

This seemed to satisfy the dispatcher, and after he hung up, he told Martha that the police were on their way.

"Good," she said. "I hope they didn't kill Dick. He may not be the nicest guy around, but he doesn't deserve to die."

This was the first time she had ever expressed her doubts about Dick's fitness as a man and a neighbor. "What do you mean, he's not the nicest guy?" he asked.

"Well, remember that trip you took last fall to visit your sister? And I was alone here for the weekend? Dick invited me over for dinner. And when I told him it didn't feel right to me, having dinner with him without my husband, he said I should loosen up."

"Loosen up!"

"He also said he wouldn't mind assisting me in some of that loosening up, or whatever else I might have in mind. It wasn't hard to know what *he* had in mind, so I brushed him off. You just don't say stuff like that to a happily married woman."

Grover turned pensive. He suddenly felt sorry that he had called the police. Maybe he should have told that gorilla to go and dance on Dick's face instead. Make sure the man was good and dead. With neighbors like that, who needed enemies?

CHAPTER 31

I had been watching that big dog for a couple of minutes and wondering how to get out of our predicament. Finally, I only saw one course of action that was open to me. And since I didn't think my friends would necessarily agree with me, and I didn't trust myself not to get cold feet, I decided to simply act now and think later. And so I jumped from that tree, aiming for the dog's head.

I don't know if you've ever had a fairly sizable cat land on your head from a height of around thirty feet? There is a law in physics that tells of objects gaining speed when they fall from a great height, and there must have been something to it, for by the time I reached the dog, my speed was such that I sort of bounced off him and then back on my four paws. And when I glanced over my shoulder as I was making my getaway, I saw that he was looking at me with a sort of dazed expression in his eyes. I could practically see the little tweetie birds flying all around his head.

Unfortunately, he was made of pretty stern stuff, and by the time I was going well and speeding up, he was up and about, and giving chase.

"Zoinks!" I said, and doubled my pace to try and stay ahead. Cats are built for the sprint, not the marathon, so it wasn't long before I was feeling the strain. Fortunately for me, a nearby hedge provided me with the perfect cover. Or so I hoped. And as I jumped the fence, suddenly I found myself face to face with an old man carrying a large pair of shears in his hands and wearing an expression of extreme surprise on his face.

"Well, I'll be damned," he managed to say before I flew past him and hid underneath a nearby sun lounger, hoping my ruse would bear fruit.

The dog simply jumped the fence and landed on all fours on the other side, looking dazed for a moment and shaking his head. But then he caught sight of me and came stalking over, wearing a pretty vicious expression!

"Get out of here, you stupid mutt!" said the man whose garden I had invaded. "Get!" he added for good measure, in case the dog hadn't understood him the first time.

Raxo didn't seem to care too much about this pesky human. He had his sights set on me—a nice juicy prey—and he wasn't going to let this old man spoil the fun. And as he slowly approached, I sat there, more or less frozen in fear while I searched around for another convenient tree to hide in. I saw plenty of rosebushes and a very nice and smooth lawn, cut to perfection, but no trees anywhere in the vicinity.

Suddenly, Raxo was upon me, and as I sat there, stiff as a board, awaiting the inevitable, suddenly a hand stole out above our heads and poured a large glass of some cooling liquid all over the vicious dog's head. It was a pink drink, I saw, and it smelled very sweet. Ice cubes tinkled and tumbled from the glass onto Raxo's head.

He didn't seem to enjoy the experience, and the unexpected shower certainly did a lot to diminish his fervor, for he produced a sound that can only be described as a high-pitched whine, and scurried off with his tail between his legs.

A face now appeared, and as I saw it upside down from my vantage point, I couldn't immediately determine who the face belonged to. Humans look very different when seen upside-down. But whatever she looked like, she was wonderful—my savior!

"Hello there," said the face, which was smiling now. "That was one nasty dog, wasn't it, kitty cat?"

"It sure was," I told the face.

"Let's get you out from under there," said the face, and proceeded to liberate me from my untenable position under the sun lounger. When viewed with the right side up, I saw that the face belonged to a very kind lady who was more than happy to give up her place on the lounger so I could recover from my recent ordeal.

"You rest easy now," she said. "That dog won't be back for you. And if he does, I'll give him another shower. I've got plenty of cosmopolitans left in the fridge."

"Thanks, miss," I said. "Thank you so much."

She had probably saved my life, and as I lay there, I gave her hand a nudge, the best way I know to express my eternal gratitude. And I probably would have stuck around for a while if I hadn't suddenly remembered why I had escaped in the first place.

Odelia! I had to warn her about this gang!

And so I thanked my benefactor once again, and then I was off, this time without a dog hot on my trail, but with a definite mission in mind.

My friends were still up that tree, unless they had seen their chance to escape while Raxo was trying to murder me. But as I glanced over my shoulder as I traversed the backyard of this nice couple, I saw that the three of them were still high up in the tree. They waved at me and I waved back.

"Go, Max!" said Harriet. "Go go go!"
I had every intention of doing just that!

CHAPTER 32

Even though Odelia had told Max to keep an eye on her grandmother for her, she still couldn't resist taking a more active role in the investigation of what exactly was going on at the home of Dick Bernstein. And so she had asked her husband to stake out the house and make sure that nothing bad happened to her gran, or her cats for that matter.

And so it was that as she and Chase sat in an unmarked car across the street from the Bernstein place, they saw several members of the Gray Panthers arrive, as Chase called them. Or at least that's what they thought they were. All of them were sprightly for their age, and fit the description to a T. As Chase took pictures and sent them to her uncle to check the database, the reports that came back from the chief weren't encouraging.

"All of them got criminal records," said Chase. "Dating back decades. It's the Gray Panthers, all right. A bunch of hardened criminals with rap sheets longer than my arm."

"And my cats are in there with them," said Odelia, getting

more and more worried about Max and the others. "And my grandmother and Scarlett."

"And let's not forget about Dick and Rock Horowitz," said Chase.

"I still wonder if they're also members of the Gray Panthers," said Odelia. "Or if they just happened to get involved because of some coincidence."

"I didn't know your grandmother's last name was Coincidence," Chase quipped.

"Ha ha," she said. "She does have a tendency to get involved in all kinds of stuff she probably shouldn't."

"Babe, your grandmother is a magnet for trouble. Whatever trouble is out there, it will find her and she will find *it*."

"So what should we do? Raid the place, like you suggested?"

Another car drove up, and this one was of the more luxurious variety.

"What do we have here?" asked Chase as he snapped a couple of shots of the car's license plate and also of the driver as he got out.

"But... I know this man," said Odelia. "That's Lonnie Love."

"Who's Lonnie Love?"

"A dog whisperer. He's famous."

"Not famous enough," said Chase. "Since I've never heard of the guy."

"He's got a show on television," she said as she quickly Googled him and showed the pictures to her husband.

"Yep, that's him all right. I wonder what a dog whisperer is doing with a gang of old crooks."

The famous TV celebrity was accompanied by a very large dog. He looked pretty vicious, she thought, and was of the Rottweiler variety. "Oh, dear. My cats are not going to like this."

"We better get in there," said Chase. "Before things get out of hand."

And so he put in a call to her uncle to ask the man's permission to raid the place. He said he'd have a team of officers at their disposal, but needed to get a warrant first, and that could take a little while. And as they sat tight, with Odelia chewing her lip in distress, a call came in. It was her uncle.

"Yep, boss," said Chase.

"One of Dick's neighbors just called nine-one-one," said Odelia's uncle. "He claims that Dick has been thrown out of an upstairs window by a man who looks like a gorilla. Also Rock Horowitz. Both men are down for the count and could very well be dead. I think you better get in there. I'm done waiting for that warrant. Probable cause is good enough for me. Backup will be there in five."

"God," she said. "I hope Gran is all right."

"Your grandmother is one of those people who are very hard to kill," said Uncle Alec. "And if that neighbor hadn't sworn that it was a large mean son of a gun doing the throwing, I would have assumed it was her that tried to murder Dick and Rock." And with these words, he hung up.

"We'll have to sit tight for five more minutes," said Chase. "Best we don't go in there without backup."

She nodded. "I know," she said nervously. Things were quickly escalating, and she was afraid of what they would find once they entered the house. Dick and Rock—dead? Her cats—victims of that vicious dog? Her grandmother and Scarlett? Who knew? Those five minutes felt like five hours. And then suddenly she saw Max sprint across the road!

"Max!" she yelled from the window. "Over here!"

The cat jumped into the car—from the street straight through the car window in one jump! Something she had never seen him do—ever. It told her how worked up he was.

"Dick and Rock had been thrown from a window," he said, panting. "And a dog whisperer is there to buy the Nazi art from a man named German Kilburn, the leader of the Gray Panthers. And the pendant that was stolen last night from the Elfords is upstairs under Gran's bed. And Dooley, Harriet, and Brutus are up in a tree. I was also in the tree but I jumped on top of Raxo's head."

"Raxo?"

"The meanest, nastiest dog I've ever seen! A real killing machine! He belongs to the dog whisperer." He placed a paw on her arm and gazed up at her with urgent fervor. "You have to save them, Odelia. They want to throw Gran out of the window too!"

"That's it," she said, opening the door of the car.

"Where are you going?" asked Chase. "Backup hasn't arrived yet."

"I'm done waiting for backup!" she said. "We have to save Gran now—or she will be dead and so will the cats and Scarlett!"

Chase nodded and also got out of the car. He started to put on his bulletproof vest and also threw her one. She put it on and accepted the gun he handed her. Backup or no backup, they needed to end this now, before this gang made more casualties.

Moments later, they were hurrying across the road in the direction of the house. Her heart was hammering in her chest, but she knew they had to end this, come what may.

CHAPTER 33

I followed from a distance as my brave humans went into the house to stop any more crimes from being committed. I would have taken a more active role, but unfortunately, there were no bulletproof vests for cats available, and also no weapons that I could have carried. Also, I didn't want to get in their way as they breached the front door. Backup would arrive imminently, but at least Chase and Odelia could make sure that Gran and Scarlett were safe and wouldn't also be hurt by the members of the Gray Panthers.

My main concern was my three friends and that vicious attack dog belonging to the so-called dog whisperer. And since I had already made that dog's acquaintance, I was careful not to run foul of him again.

The moment my humans entered the house, chaos broke out, with the members of the Gray Panthers all fleeing through the window and into the backyard, as was to be expected. Crooks are notoriously shy people and don't enjoy mingling with the police when they can avoid it. The only person who didn't run away was the dog whisperer, but that was mainly because Chase had a gun pointed at him and made it clear that he wouldn't hesitate to use it if the man got involved in 'any funny business.'

I hurried out the door and to the tree where my three friends were still holed up, and was surprised to find that they must have left, for there was no sign of any of them. There was a sort of ruckus nearby, and when I looked over, I saw that Brutus had attached himself to the pants leg of one Gray Panther, Harriet to the arm of a second one, and Dooley to the calf of a third. The three remaining Gray Panthers were trying their darndest to liberate their friends of the three cats, and a jolly old time was had by all.

And since I didn't want to let them do all the dirty work, I jumped into the fray and accosted the leader of the Gray Panthers, who had been trying to remove Brutus from his friend's leg. Oddly enough, of the big dog belonging to the dog whisperer, there was not a single trace. But then I saw that he was sitting on top of Dick and was sniffing at the latter's hair for some reason.

The melee or fracas the four of us were involved in lasted until a group of officers came running out of the house and placed the Gray Panthers under arrest. Backup had finally arrived, and they didn't disappoint.

"Good," said Brutus as he spat something on the lawn that looked like a piece of pants. "That guy tasted really bad."

"Mine tasted like old socks," said Harriet, which surprised me, since I have no idea what old socks taste like, having never tried them.

"Mine tasted like chicken," Dooley said. "But not in a good way."

"What did yours taste like, Max?" asked Harriet.

"Well," I said, "I don't really know. But he smelled like bleach."

"They all smelled like bleach," said Harriet with a grimace.

We returned to the house and gathered around Dick and Rock, still lying prone on the lawn, with Raxo sitting atop them, looking like the victor of some bloody conflict.

"These men are mine," he growled menacingly. "These are the spoils, and the spoils are mine! And I ain't sharing!" He gave me a dirty look. "That was a nasty trick you played on me, cat. Pouring that stuff on top of my head. And I have to admit you took me by surprise. But that won't happen to me a second time."

"It was some kind of cocktail," I told the dog. "The lady called it a cosmopolitan."

"It was fruity," he admitted as he licked at his snout. "Very refreshing."

"Did you pour a cocktail on his head?" asked Brutus.

"I didn't, but one of Dick's neighbors did," I said.

"Nasty trick to play on a dog," Raxo lamented. "Not fair. But then what else can you expect from a cat? You guys never play fair and square, do you? Always escaping in trees and asking other people to do your dirty work for you."

"I didn't ask anyone to do my dirty work for me," I said. "But you have to admit that it wasn't very nice of you to try and catch us. I mean, what did we ever do to you?"

He gave me a look of surprise. "What do you mean, what did you ever do to me?"

"You attacked us without provocation! That was very mean-spirited of you, Raxo."

He gave me a thoughtful look. "It's an instinct."

"And your human never taught you to fight that instinct?"

"No, he didn't. On the contrary. He always told me to follow my instinct."

"Lousy dog whisperer he is," said Harriet.

The dog eyed her with a touch of menace. "Do you really want to go down that route, cat? Hurl these nasty slurs at me? I could go for another round, you know? Can you?"

Harriet held up her paw. "No, that's fine, Raxo."

"I thought so." He glanced down at Dick, who was stirring now. "Hey, looks like this one is still alive," he said with a note of surprise in his voice.

Dick sat up, shifting the dog from his back. He touched his head. "What happened?" he asked. But then his eyes focused, and he saw me, and groaned. "Not you guys again!"

"I'm sorry," I said as he sneezed once, twice, and then a third time in quick succession. "But let me just say that I'm glad that you're not dead, Dick."

His friend Rock now also stirred and groaned. As he sat up, he rubbed his shoulder and asked, "What happened? I feel like I've been thrown from a window."

"We *were* thrown from the window," said Dick.

"I feel like I've broken a couple of bones," said Rock.

"Same here. German is definitely not my friend anymore."

"If I had known he liked to throw people out of windows…"

Gran and Scarlett came wandering out of the house, which was now crawling with police officers. "You guys are still alive?" asked Gran, sounding surprised.

"No thanks to you!" said Dick. "First you bring these cats of yours, even though you know full well I'm allergic, and then you get us involved in this crazy gang!"

"Hey, German Kilburn is *your* friend," Gran reminded Dick.

"Yeah, I know. I should learn to pick my friends more wisely."

"Good thing he's your friend, Dick," said Scarlett. "Thanks to you, the Gray Panthers have all been arrested, and the things they stole from the museum have all been found."

"And the dog whisperer has also been arrested," Gran added.

"What dog whisperer?" asked Rock, having a hard time following the plot.

"Keep up, will you, Rock?" said Gran. "Lonnie Love is a famous dog whisperer, but what was less known is that he's also a big collector of Nazi art. He's the buyer Dick's buddy German Kilburn had lined up."

"Well, he ain't my buddy anymore," said Dick. "Not after telling his goon to throw me out of the window." He rubbed his elbow. "Ouch. I think something is broken."

Odelia and Chase came walking out of the house. Odelia seemed relieved that we were all fine, even though Rock and Dick were a little banged up. But nothing that a stay at the hospital wouldn't fix. To that purpose, an ambulance had been called and would soon arrive to take these two new recruits of the neighborhood watch to the hospital. Though I had a feeling that their first time joining the watch was also the last time. What can I say? Not everybody can take the heat!

"Did you find the loot?" asked Gran.

"We did," said Odelia. "We found everything that was stolen yesterday. The museum people will be over the moon."

"And so will Pinkie," I said.

"Who's Pinkie?" asked Raxo.

"She's a little doggie that belongs to one of the museum guards," I said.

"A dog?" asked Raxo, his ears pricking up.

"The sweetest dog in the world," I told him.

"The polar opposite of you, in other words," Harriet said.

Chase now walked up to the dog and studied him for a moment. "We should probably call a dog handler," he said.

For the first time, Raxo seemed to understand that his life might get a lot more complicated now that his human had been arrested. "What's going to happen to me?" he asked.

"I'm not sure," I said. "Does Lonnie have relatives who can take care of you? A brother or a sister, maybe?"

"They all live in Switzerland," said Raxo. "And they all hate me." He sagged a little, and I saw that the fight had gone completely out of him. "Don't send me to the pound," he said. "I hate it at the pound. I was there before Lonnie adopted me, and it was the worst time of my life."

I glanced up at Odelia and told her what Raxo had told us. She gave me a thoughtful look. "He tried to bite you, didn't he? Was extremely aggressive towards you guys?"

"He was only trying to protect his human, I'm sure," said Brutus.

"Yeah, he was only being a loyal dog," said Dooley.

"He's not so bad," said Harriet.

Odelia smiled. "That's very noble of you guys. But it's not up to us. It will all depend on what happens to Lonnie Love."

"Whatever happens to me," said Raxo, "I'm resigned to my fate." And then he placed his head on his front paws and licked his lips. "Do I taste strawberry?"

Dooley sniffed the Rottweiler. "Cranberry and lime," he said determinedly.

The dog smiled. "Okay, cat. Cranberry and lime it is."

"Dooley," said Dooley. "And these are Max, Harriet, and Brutus."

"Good to put a name to your prey, isn't it, dog?" asked Brutus.

"Raxo. And I never considered you guys prey. More like playmates. Buddies to have some fun with. And I gotta say, you guys gave as good as you got. Worthy opponents."

"You too, Raxo," I said. "A very worthy opponent."

When we bumped fists with the big dog, both Dick and Rock seemed surprised. Then Dick said, "Those cats of yours are just about the weirdest cats I've ever seen, Vesta."

Gran smiled. "Thanks, Dick. That's probably the nicest thing you've ever said to me."

CHAPTER 34

Tex had fired up the grill, and Marge had brought out the potato salad, and the family were all waiting expectantly for the feast that was about to unfold in the couple's backyard. Not least of those participants were the four of us, who had taken up position on the porch swing and were in eager anticipation of some tasty morsels coming our way.

Tex had told us he wanted to reward us for a job well done, even though we hadn't done much. It was actually Gran who was the hero of the hour, as even her son had to admit that without her infiltrating the gang of the Gray Panthers, they would have probably gotten away with their crime and might have already left the country by now.

Her perspicacity, and of course the fact that Dick was an old acquaintance of the gang leader, had led her to thwart their plans and return the stolen loot. Lonnie would be punished for his role in the heist and also for the theft of the pendant from the Elfords.

Morris and Lindsey had been over the moon to learn that the pendant that had been languishing in one of their drawers for years was actually a priceless piece that belonged in a museum. They had already been fielding offers to have it sold at auction.

"I still don't understand how the Gray Panthers knew that the pendant was in the possession of the Elfords," said Harriet.

"Coincidence," I said. "One of the Gray Panthers' cousins works as a plumber, and he had a lucrative sideline in that he liked to scope out places he visited, looking for stuff that might be of interest to his cousin. During a recent job at the Elfords' house, he happened upon the pendant and took a picture. It was enough to set in motion a sequence of events that led to this outcome. German Kilburn knew he had struck gold and immediately contacted Lonnie Love, who had bought things from him in the past. The pendant was the big prize, though. Something he had been looking for for years."

"How did it end up in the Elfords' house?"

"That," I said, "is something for historians to thresh out, but as I understood, it may have had something to do with the fact that Lindsey Elford's side of the family is Russian. And as we all know, the Russians were first on the scene of the bunker where Adolf Hitler and his mistress Eva Braun died. Possibly some of their possessions traveled to Russia, and from there made their way to Lindsey. It's possible we will never know, but at least the piece has been found and will hopefully end up in a museum."

"What's going to happen to Raxo now, Max?" asked Dooley.

"Oh, didn't you know? He's been adopted by Harold for the time being. At least until Lonnie Love is released from prison." Harold felt for the dog. Being a dog person, he didn't think it was fair that Raxo had to suffer because his human was a crook. And so he had taken Raxo home on trial, to see if he got along with Pinkie. And as it turned out, Pinkie took to Raxo from the start, and vice versa. The two were good friends now.

"Let's hope Raxo will be nice to Pinkie," said Dooley. "Especially after he was so vicious to us."

"Pinkie seems to have a great influence on him," I said. "She even told me when we paid Harold a visit at the museum that she's been teaching him to be a guard dog."

"I can't imagine there's a lot about being a guard dog Raxo has to learn," said Brutus. "That dog was born to guard."

"Which is exactly why Harold is over the moon with his new acquisition."

"Ironic, isn't it?" said Harriet. "The dog belonging to the man who ordered the heist is now guarding the museum."

"Which is exactly how it should be," I said.

"You know," said Gran, as she pronged a piece of potato salad, "I was thinking about expanding the neighborhood watch. After the success we had and the attention we got in the papers, people have been begging us to sign up."

"We've been getting a lot of candidates," Scarlett confirmed. "Lots of people want to be watch members."

"What about Dick and Rock?" asked Charlene. "I thought they were new watch members."

Gran grimaced. "Dick and Rock quit. Too stressful and too dangerous. Though I don't see what's dangerous about it. And stressful? It's a barrel of laughs, that's what it is."

"And gratifying," said Scarlett.

"Absolutely. What could be more gratifying than protecting people's lives and personal property? It's an honor to be able to serve our community like this."

Chase jerked his thumb at the field located behind the backyard. "Any news on this front? We're getting a lot of complaints about youths using the shack as a drug den."

"We've got some good news in regards to that," said Charlene. "The town council is considering several options to develop the field. So it looks as if we'll finally be able to get rid of this eyesore and build something the whole community can enjoy."

"A park?" asked Odelia.

"Condos?" asked Gran.

"An amusement park?" asked Grace.

"Or a new town hall!" said Charlene proudly. But when she saw the disappointed faces, she laughed. "Just kidding! Nothing has been decided yet. There are several options on the table, but the community will have the final word. We will organize a town hall meeting, and everyone will be invited to give ideas and suggestions. We will sort through all of them, and the most popular—and feasible—will win, I promise."

"I hope it's a park," said Odelia happily.

"And I hope it's condos," said Gran. "Maybe I'll buy one."

For some strange reason, she had stopped sleepwalking, and so that gate at the top of the stairs had been removed. And since Dick had pretty much kicked her out of the house, and Scarlett had expressed a certain reluctance to live with her good friend, Gran had moved back home. Which was good news for Dooley, who had hated it when his human moved out. Us cats like things just so, and too much change makes us anxious.

"I hope it's an amusement park," said Grace. "Like Disneyland, you know. Though smaller, of course. But with plenty of fun rides. I'd visit the park every day!"

"I wouldn't mind if it stayed exactly the way it is right now," said Dooley. "I mean, where are the mice going to go, Max? They won't have a place to live anymore. Or the shrews. Or the ants. Or the rabbits and all the other creatures. It's not fair to them, is it?"

"They should turn it into a nature reserve," said Harriet. "That way we can all enjoy it. Every species equally served."

"Even the drug addicts?" asked Brutus.

"Well," said Harriet thoughtfully. "I mean, they're creatures too, aren't they? Though it's true that they cause plenty of trouble for all involved. So maybe let's draw the line there. All creatures are welcome, except drug addicts."

And on that note, Tex started doling out the goodies, and we all tucked in.

"There's one thing that isn't clear to me, Max," said Brutus. "Who shot Kurt?"

I smiled. "That was Willie."

"The guy who threw Dick and Rock out of the window?"

"One and the same. His full name is Willie Brocklesby, and German had told him to stake out the Elfords' place, hoping to break in and steal that pendant."

"Was it also him that ran into Gran?" asked Dooley.

"Yep. But when he saw that she didn't pose a threat, he left her alone."

"So why didn't he leave Kurt alone?" asked Harriet.

"Willie had forgotten his sweater in the field the night before, during his stakeout. He had returned to get it back when he saw that Kurt was rifling through its pockets and found the necklace that was a gift from Willie's daughter, who passed away a couple of years ago. He didn't like to see a stranger pawing his precious necklace, so he shot him."

"Shoot first, ask questions later," said Brutus.

"Not a nice man, Max," said Dooley.

"No, you can say that again," I agreed.

"What about the bleach?" asked Harriet.

I shrugged. "What can I say? I guess Willie is a crook, but he's a clean crook." All of the Gray Panthers had a predilection for bleach, since they believed it removed fingerprints but also DNA, and kept them safe from being identified by the cops.

"At least Kurt will be all right," said Harriet.

After the scare our neighbor had at the hospital, he had been recovering just fine and would return home any day now. Fifi was over the moon, and so was Gilda, and the neighborhood had organized a welcome home party. It would warm the cockles of the old curmudgeon's heart. Harriet had offered to sing a song, but that had been rejected by the organizing committee. I had a sneaking suspicion it was Gran who had done the rejecting, but since Harriet couldn't prove it, there was nothing she could do.

"I'm going to sing anyway," she now told us.

"What are you talking about?" I asked as I savored the piece of chicken Tex had placed in front of me.

"When Kurt arrives home? I know Gran doesn't want me to sing."

"You can't prove that," I said.

"I know it was her, Max!" she said. "Who else could it have been? She's the only one who knew I planned to sing a song for Kurt. And she's also the only one on that committee who can talk to me. Anyway, it doesn't matter. I don't need her permission. I will sing when I want to sing, and I'm going to give Kurt the benefit of my gift."

Brutus and I shared a look of alarm. "What are you going to sing?" asked Brutus.

"I haven't decided yet, but something by Celine, probably."

We both gulped. Whenever Harriet sings a song by her favorite singer, window panes rattle, doors tremble out of their hinges, eardrums bleed, and generally mayhem ensues.

"Um... maybe you should take it easy on Kurt," I said. "The man has been shot, Harriet. He needs to rest."

She gave me a dirty look. "I see. You also don't want me to sing, is that it?"

"Oh, no, absolutely not!" I assured her. "Of course I want you to sing. It's just that Kurt needs to rest. And so listening to your beautiful voice may be too much for him."

She thought for a moment. "You know, Max, you may have a point. He might get so overwhelmed with emotion when he listens to me that it's going to tax his old heart. No, you're absolutely right. I should probably wait a couple of days until he's well and truly recovered before I expose him to the sheer beauty of my voice."

"Or a couple of weeks," I suggested.

"Or months," Brutus added. "Best not to take any chances," he added.

She nodded. "Okay, I have decided. I will wait. Kurt is a sick man and he needs his strength before he can truly appreciate the amazing talent that is Harriet."

"Who is this second Harriet, Harriet?" asked Dooley.

"I was referring to myself in the third person, Dooley. Any diva does. And this diva is as much a diva as the next diva."

"Which diva?" he asked, looking confused.

"Any diva!"

Diva or no diva, she had certainly been instrumental in capturing this gang of Gray Panthers. As it turned out, both the butt and the bud had belonged to the Panthers. DNA was found on the cigarette butt that was linked to German Kilburn, and the hearing aid had belonged to Baldie, whose real name was Gustavo Horwill and who was an old computer hacker whose hearing wasn't what it used to be.

I had eaten my fill and pushed my plate away. Time to take a nap, I decided. It had been a pretty trying couple of days, and I needed a prolonged nap to get me back in shape. And I had just closed my eyes when Dooley gave me a nudge.

"I'm sleeping, Dooley," I informed him.

"I hope they build a park, Max. That way, cat choir can move here and we don't have to go to Hampton Cove Park every night."

I looked up in alarm. "You mean... dozens of cats traipsing all over our neighborhood every night? Walking in and out of our home? Eating our kibble? Using our litter box?"

"Exactly! All of our friends paying us a visit every night! Sounds great, doesn't it?"

I gulped. It sounded more like a nightmare to me than a dream come true. Maybe I should throw my own idea in the hat. The idea that they should probably keep Blake's Field exactly the way it was. Like Dooley, I like things to stay the way they are. And there's nothing wrong with that. Nothing wrong with tradition.

Well, except maybe the drug people. Harriet was right. That was one species of creature we could definitely do without. But apart from them, I liked Blake's Field as a refuge for any creature that needed a break from the world. Like the three colonies of mice that had made their home there, or the ant colony, or the shrews. In fact many of our friends now lived in that field, and as far as I was concerned, they could stay there.

I closed my eyes again and was soon sleeping peacefully. And I would have slept on if a poke in the ribs hadn't alerted me that someone desired speech with me. When I opened my eyes, I saw that it was none other than Pinkie and Raxo!

They had brought their human, Harold Hudspith, along, who looked a little nervous when he surveyed the scene. But Marge quickly put him at ease and offered him a chair, while Tex pressed a plate into his hands that was loaded with tasty goodies.

"So nice of your humans to invite us, Max," said Pinkie.

"Good to see you guys again," said Raxo. He seemed to have mellowed out a great deal since our adventure at Dick's place.

"So, how are things?" I asked.

"Oh, fine, fine," said Raxo. "I thought I would miss Switzerland, but as it turns out, I don't miss it at all. Howard is such a great guy, and of course Pinkie is simply the best and made me feel right at home." He smiled. "In hindsight, maybe what happened was a good thing, you know. Life is a lot simpler now. No more selfies, no more dog shows, no more TV appearances. And I have to say I like it. Life lived at a slower pace suits me just fine." He placed a paw on my shoulder and gave me a penetrating look. I felt a little uncomfortable and was already starting to gauge the distance to the nearest tree. But I shouldn't have worried. The Rottweiler's days of chasing cats across the lawn were over. "I wanted to thank you for asking Howard if I could stay with him, Max. If not for you, I would have been shipped off to the nearest pound, and I would probably be languishing there, as not many people are eager to adopt a mean old Rottweiler like me."

"Don't mention it, Raxo," I said warmly. "I'm glad things worked out for you."

And since Pinkie and Raxo were also treasured guests, Tex came hurrying up with more plates to feed the two dogs. As we watched how Raxo stowed away a ton of food, I wondered if we hadn't done Harold a disservice by foisting this big dog on him. The fellow could eat for two! But as Harold told the collected members of my family how he adored Raxo, I shouldn't have worried. He clearly was crazy about the big old mutt.

Raxo slobbered his way through the pile of food and licked his lips as he settled back. "And now for dessert," he said, "I think I'll have one of you guys." He grinned until his incisors shone, and when we all gave him a look of uncertainty, he laughed. "I'm sorry. That wasn't funny, was it?"

"No, it wasn't," said Harriet. "Jokes like that won't make you popular around here, Raxo."

"Just kidding," he said. "Though I could use some exercise, you know."

Brutus smiled. "What did you have in mind?"

And so, just for old time's sake, and to work off the big meal we had devoured, we reenacted the same game we had played over at Dick's house. Only we took it to the field behind the house instead. Okay, so kids like to play cops and robbers, so why shouldn't we play cats and dogs? Rufus and Fifi also joined in, and it has to be said we had a great time until, as was probably to be expected when cats play with dogs, the four of us found ourselves up in a tree with Raxo, Pinkie, Rufus and Fifi barking up a storm down below. When push comes to shove, you just can't beat instinct, can you?

THE END

Thanks for reading! If you want to know when a new Nic Saint book comes out, sign up for Nic's mailing list: nicsaint.com/news

EXCERPT FROM PURRFECT SPIDER (MAX 90)

Chapter One

I had been eyeing Dooley for a while and thought that he didn't look as good as he should. It made me wonder if he could be ill. But since I didn't want to cause concern, and I knew how much my friend hates those visits to the vet, I didn't think it was prudent to clothe my thoughts in words, and so I figured I might simply observe him for a couple of days to see if his condition improved. If not, I saw no other recourse but to tell Odelia. But since essentially I'm an optimistic type of kitty, I was hopeful Dooley would soon rally.

Cats do sometimes get these off-days, just like humans. We go off our feed, or catch some bug, and it immediately shows in the state of our fur. Humans go pale and look as if they're at death's door, we look as if we've stopped grooming ourselves, which we have.

It's a natural process and I knew I shouldn't read too much into it. And as I closed my eyes again, I thought that maybe I should talk to Harriet, who is very sensitive about such things as personal appearance. Maybe she would have a

EXCERPT FROM PURRFECT SPIDER (MAX 90)

few tips to make Dooley look right as rain again. After all, it could be a simple case of not getting enough sleep, or some personal issue he was struggling with. Dooley might be my best friend, but that doesn't necessarily mean he confides in me about everything that's going on with him.

"Max?" he asked suddenly.

"Mh?" I said, my eyes immediately flashing open again.

"That spider…"

"What spider?"

We were lying on the deck, and as far as I could tell there were no spiders anywhere in the vicinity, nor should there be, as Odelia hates spiders and has made a deal with her husband that he will always evict them from the premises the moment he spots one.

"I met a spider the other day," he confessed. "It was in Tex's garden shed. We got to talking, and he told me a few things that I thought were interesting but also concerning."

"What did he tell you?" I asked, relaxing again.

If Odelia spots a spider that has escaped her husband's scrutiny, she has a habit of screaming the house down, especially when it's one of those big and hairy specimens. And I have to confess I'm not a big fan of the species either.

"Well, he told me that very soon now, there's going to be some very big changes."

"What changes?"

"I'm not sure," said Dooley, making a face. "Though I got the impression that he knew exactly what was going to happen, but didn't want to alarm me."

"He was probably talking through his hat. Trying to be the big man on campus."

"But he wasn't wearing a hat, Max," said Dooley, giving me a look of confusion. "And he wasn't very big either. And I met him in the shed, not a campus."

"It's just an expression, Dooley," I said. "It means he

doesn't know what he's saying. Just making conversation, you know, and trying to get your attention."

"Well, he got my attention, all right," said Dooley. "I don't think I would like things to change. In fact, I like things just the way they are."

"Me too," I said as I closed my eyes again. "I like everything exactly the way it is right now. So let's not jinx things by talking about any possible changes, shall we?"

"No, let's not," said Dooley.

Harriet and Brutus, who had been traipsing around in the field behind the house, came walking up. "You guys," said Brutus, sounding out of breath. "Did you see those spiders?"

"What spiders?" I asked, my eyes flashing open again. This was too much of a coincidence. "Where?"

"By the old shack," said Brutus. "It's full of spiders back there. They're all over the place, and spread out across the field. Everywhere you go, you can see their webs. It's freaky."

I shivered. I don't enjoy walking through the field and getting those spiderwebs on me. It's uncomfortable, and frankly a little rude, I always find, for spiders to leave their webs hanging around like that. "They should be more careful where they put those things," I said.

"There's even a place in the field where it's almost impossible to go now," said Brutus. "It's one giant thick spiderweb, with thousands of little spiders crawling all over it. I don't like to venture there, and I'm not even afraid of spiders."

"You should be," said Harriet. "Some spiders can bite you pretty bad, and others are poisonous, did you know?"

"I'm sure there are no poisonous spiders here in Hampton Cove," said Brutus with a laugh. "That's more the Amazon or Australia or any of those places. Our climate is too cold for poisonous species of spiders to thrive here."

"And I'm telling you that they're here," said Harriet. "Even Shanille told me last night that Father Reilly had a parish-

EXCERPT FROM PURRFECT SPIDER (MAX 90)

ioner who was bitten by a spider and he developed the most gruesome rash on his neck. It was as big as a bird's egg and was all red and swollen. In the end, he had to go to the hospital, and they said that if he hadn't gone, he might have died."

"That sounds like an urban legend," said Brutus. "No spider can cause that kind of rash. Not here in Hampton Cove anyway."

"Suit yourself. If you don't want to believe me, that's up to you. I'm just telling you what Shanille told me, and as we all know, Shanille wouldn't make up a story like that. It's against her faith."

That was true enough. As a staunch Catholic, Shanille doesn't believe in making up stories simply to impress people. She believes in telling it like it is, which might get awkward if the person she's talking about is also the person she's talking *to*.

"Look, I'm sure it's just a phase," I said. "A seasonal thing, you know. Pretty soon they will all be gone again."

"Yeah, as soon as the weather turns and the temperatures drop, this spider business will be a thing of the past," said Brutus.

"I wouldn't be so sure about that," said Harriet, who was starting to sound more and more like an alarmist, I thought. "These spiders are here to stay, and if that's true, we'll simply have to start being a lot more careful, and also our humans. And I'm thinking specifically about Grace and Gran, who are both very vulnerable to this sort of threat."

"Would you call it a threat?" I asked.

"I most certainly would," said Harriet, causing Dooley to give me a look of concern.

"Maybe this is the big change my friend the spider was talking about," he said.

"You are friends with a spider?" asked Harriet.

"I met him a couple of days ago. He hangs out in Tex's

garden shed, and he told me that big changes are coming. He wouldn't tell me what those changes were, though."

"Probably this spider invasion," said Harriet, nodding. "Better ask your friend to be more specific, Dooley," she advised. "We need to make sure that we are not attacked by these monsters. If there are thousands and thousands of them out there, and only four of us, you can see how that's going to pose a major problem, can't you?"

I gulped a little. All this talk about thousands of spiders was affecting my capacity to enjoy a nice and peaceful nap, but when I told Harriet, she didn't agree.

"It isn't alarmist to prepare yourself for a contingency you know is coming, Max," she said. "It's simply common sense."

Common sense or not, if those spiders started spreading to the backyard and then to the house, I would advise our humans to stock up on spider repellant—and plenty of it!

Chapter Two

Clark Timberlake looked through his viewfinder and shook his head. It still wasn't what he was looking for. He'd been scouting for a great location for his next project for weeks, and even though he had a feeling he was close, being the perfectionist that he was, he knew he could do better. And so he studied the list of possible locations his assistants had jotted down and saw that the next possibility was just around the corner. He needed a house that looked normal enough from the outside but at the same time had a sort of spooky vibe. It was subtle, but it was what he needed and he was going to get it, however long it took him.

He walked the distance to the street that was next on the list, and when he arrived there, he had to admit that he liked what he saw. In fact, he liked it a lot. It was an ordinary house like you could find on any street, on any block,

EXCERPT FROM PURRFECT SPIDER (MAX 90)

in any suburb, but there was something about it that was… off. He couldn't really put his finger on it, but this house had a history. It had suffered. It had gone through the wringer. And since that was exactly what he needed to convey, he put the viewfinder to his eye and studied the house intently.

As he did, he got a chill. A vibe that told him that he had found what he was looking for. As he stared at the place, a cat walked out from behind the house and settled on the small stone wall that had been erected in front of the house and started licking itself. Just then, the cat, a big fat orange specimen, glanced up in his direction and their eyes locked.

Another shiver, more pronounced this time. Goosebumps up and down his arms.

"You," he said, pointing to the fat cat. "I want you in my movie!"

He walked up to the house, and since he didn't believe in wasting time, pressed his finger on the buzzer. Moments later, the door was opened by a beautiful young blonde.

"Hi there," he said. "My name is Clark Timberlake and I'm a movie director. How much for the house?"

She stared at him. "Excuse me?"

"Not to buy, mind you," he clarified, realizing that he probably should have let an assistant handle this part of the process. He was a little brusque in his ways of handling the delicate negotiations that were involved in dealing with people. "I want to use your house for my next movie," he explained. He then pointed to the fat cat. "Is that your cat?"

"Um, yes, as a matter of fact, it is," she said.

"I want him in my movie," he declared.

Her jaw had dropped, which he saw as a good sign.

"How much?" he asked therefore.

"How much for what?"

He frowned. He didn't like people that were a little thick.

EXCERPT FROM PURRFECT SPIDER (MAX 90)

It complicated things. "How much to use your house for my movie? And the cat, of course. Just name your price, miss."

"My house is not for sale, sir," she said. "And neither is my cat." She made to close the door, but since he had been in this position before, he hastened to place a well-shod foot in the way. He probably shouldn't have done that, for she got a sort of set look about her that he didn't think was a good sign. Then she bellowed, "Chase! Can you come here a minute!"

Moments later, a beefy giant appeared. Clark had to strain his neck to look up at the guy.

"What seems to be the problem?" the beefcake asked.

"This man here wants to buy our house, and also Max. Can you please explain to him that neither are for sale?"

"I don't want to buy anything," he said. He realized he hadn't expressed himself well. His assistants often said he was a brilliant director, but a lousy communicator. "I'm a movie director, you see. And I want to film my next movie in your house. It's not going to take long. One month at the most, maybe a little less. So all I want is to rent your house for the time of the shoot. And also that fat cat over there. I just have to have it in my movie."

The guy seemed more interested in his proposal than the dame. "You want to rent the house for a month so you can film a movie here, and also put Max in your movie?"

He nodded, happy that finally someone understood what he was trying to get across. "I told this lady to name her price."

"How about... a thousand bucks a week?" the guy said.

"Done," he said, happy at such a lowball offer. He held out his hand. "I'll have my assistant draw up the contract."

The woman gave him a look of surprise. "You're willing to pay us a thousand bucks a week so you can use our home in your movie?"

"Absolutely. I've been looking for the right house for

EXCERPT FROM PURRFECT SPIDER (MAX 90)

weeks now, and have traveled up and down Long Island. Your home is *exactly* what I need. It's got that special vibe I want."

The woman turned to the beefy fellow. "But what about us, Chase? Where are we going to live in the meantime?"

"We could stay with your mom and dad," he suggested. "If it's only for a month, we'll manage."

"And what about our furniture?"

"Oh, you don't have to worry about that," said Clark. "We'll put all of that in storage if you like. We have professional crews who deal with this kind of thing all the time. We'll remove all of your furniture, all of your furnishings and personal stuff, and put it in storage, but before we do that, we take pictures of everything. And then when the shoot is over, we put everything back exactly the way it was, down to the last detail. Wallpaper, curtains, carpeting—everything. You will get your house back exactly the way it was."

"See?" said the beefcake. "Easy money, babe. Plus bragging rights for being in a movie."

"I guess," she said, not fully convinced. She turned to Clark. "And what was that you said about Max? You want him in your movie?"

"I need a cat," he explained. "But not just any cat. I need... Max, you said his name was?"

"That's right."

"Well, I need Max in my movie," he said. "He's exactly what I had in mind."

"Will he have to... act?"

"Oh, no. No acting required whatsoever. He will simply have to walk from point A to point B, and he will also have to jump around when we tell him to. But we have professional animal trainers who will work with him."

"Max doesn't need a trainer," said the beefcake. "He'll do exactly what you tell him to. Okay, so maybe that's not

EXCERPT FROM PURRFECT SPIDER (MAX 90)

entirely true," he amended. "He will do what Odelia tells him to."

"Odelia?" asked the director.

"I'm Odelia," said the blond babe. "Odelia Kingsley. And this is my husband Chase."

"Nice to meet you," he said, even though he wasn't really interested in the couple. He didn't think he could use them in his movie, and as a consequence, they were of no importance. But then he caught on to what the big fellow said. "Max will do as you say?"

"Absolutely," said the guy. "He listens to her, you see."

"He does," said this Odelia person.

"Prove it," said Clark. "Tell him to come here."

"Max!" she bellowed, causing his ears to hurt. "Come here a moment, will you?"

Without delay, the cat jumped off the low wall and came trotting up. Now it was Clark's jaw that dropped. In all of his years working with kids and animals, he had never seen a cat respond so astutely to a command. "Can you... can you tell him to stand on his hind legs?"

"Stand on his hind legs?"

"Yeah, or make him do something? Doesn't matter what."

"Max, can you give me a paw?" asked Odelia.

And much to his astonishment, the cat did exactly that!

"Well, I'll be damned," he said, scratching his head. "I've never seen anything like it." His excitement was growing by leaps and bounds. "How much for the cat?"

"Max is not for sale," said the woman, turning sour on him again.

"I didn't mean it like that. How much to put him in my movie?"

"Well, just pay him the usual fee," said the beefcake.

"Ten thousand," he suggested off the top of his head. It was steep for a pet actor, but he had a good feeling about

Max. If the cat could pull this off, he'd be the star of the movie.

"So what does he have to do, exactly?" asked Odelia carefully.

Unlike her husband, she wasn't so easy to impress. "Well, like I said, walk from point A to point B and jump around. Things like that."

"And you're willing to pay ten thousand dollars for that?"

"It's very rare to get a cat that does what the director wants," he explained. "In fact, it's almost impossible to make them do what you want. That gag about never working with pets or kids is true for a reason. But if you can make him follow my instructions, then yeah, he's worth his weight in gold, pretty much."

She exchanged a look with her husband, and he nodded. Then she did the strangest thing. She crouched down and asked the cat! "Max, what do you say? Do you want to be in a movie?" The cat meowed up a storm for a moment, and the ditzy blonde smiled a radiant smile. "Okay," she said finally. "We'll do it. We'll be in your movie."

Chapter Three

Lily Heckley looked out of the window of her office and wondered again about the man standing across the street. He had been there for the past hour or so. Mostly he was checking his phone, an innocent enough pastime, but she had noticed that from time to time he looked up at the office, as if he was waiting for someone—or something. She shrugged and decided that she probably should get on with her job and not waste time gazing idly out of windows. She would never get through her workload that way.

The problem was that the job she had been assigned seemed so utterly and completely pointless she had a hard

EXCERPT FROM PURRFECT SPIDER (MAX 90)

time focusing on the task at hand. As a junior graphic designer of an ad agency, she had to edit the new campaign for one of their bigger clients. The problem was that she wasn't fully on board with the concept. The company, a perfume brand that had been in business for decades and had a solid reputation, had asked Ophelae to design a campaign around their new fragrance, aimed at a younger segment of the market. They had recently attracted a new CEO, who wanted to shake things up, and had asked them to design a campaign that was more daring, more appealing to the younger demographic. And so Patsy Fletcher, Ophelae's creative director, had come up with an edgy campaign that was going to shock some of the older clients but hopefully attract a lot of new ones.

Lily didn't like it, and she hadn't minced words when she had voiced this opinion in their most recent creative team meeting. But Patsy had immediately shut her down and had basically told her that her opinion didn't matter and that she should just do as she was told. She hadn't said the 'or else' part of her statement out loud, but it was implied.

And so now Lily had to spend her time working on a campaign she thought was going to alienate Fleur's existing client base, and reflect badly on Ophelae. If the new fragrance tanked, other brands might think twice before hiring Ophelae. Hopefully, it wouldn't come to that, but it might. The new campaign was dark and grungy and was a major gamble.

She sighed and got busy removing some blemishes from the face of one of the models they had hired for the shoot. The model suffered from acne, and she had a lot of work getting rid of all the pimples. The girl looked very heroine chic, the look Patsy was going for. As Lily also removed a scar from the model's leg, she felt someone standing behind her. She looked up and saw that Patsy was eyeing her with a critical expression on her face.

"What do you think you're doing?" she demanded heatedly.

"Um... cleaning up the images?" she said.

"Didn't I tell you to leave all of that in?"

"But... we always remove blemishes like these."

"Not this time. I want them all in. The scars, the acne, the tattoos, the imperfections. The more the merrier. It's all part of the campaign the client wants. He wants real people, not perfectly airbrushed models. Just make it darker."

"Darker?"

"A lot darker. We want to shock the viewer. Really make this an image that will stop the scroll," she added. "And when you're done with this, I want you to look at the static TikTok images too. They're too clean. Too... pretty."

"Yes, Patsy," she said dutifully, knowing better than to offer her personal opinion.

"Make it more rough, more edgy, more gritty. We want images that are in your face."

She nodded and reversed a couple of the changes she had made. As if by magic, all of the model's facial imperfections reappeared. The acne, the moles, the scars...

"That's better," said Patsy, well pleased. "Much better."

Lily wondered how the model would feel about this. Not everyone wanted to appear in a major nationwide campaign looking the way they did when they got out of bed in the morning. Then again, if that's what the client wanted, that's what the client would get.

She had been working for another half hour when she happened to glance out of the window again, to give her eyes a break. Great was her surprise when that same man was still standing there. As she looked down, he looked up, and their eyes met. Immediately he looked away again, obviously

EXCERPT FROM PURRFECT SPIDER (MAX 90)

feeling caught. He even walked away from the lamppost he had been leaning against and crossed the street so he would be out of sight.

How odd, she felt. But since there was no law against standing on the corner of the street looking at buildings, she put it out of her mind and returned to her work. She had just finished exporting the finished image and saving it in the cloud when suddenly there was a major explosion that rocked the building. She jumped up from her chair and reeled back. At the entrance to the office, she could see flames and a thick cloud of smoke.

Her coworkers all stared at the conflagration in horror and shock, and suddenly a loud voice rang out. "Fire exit! Now!"

It was Patsy, and the next moment they were all running to the exit on the other side of the office. Since there were at least fifty people, there was a hold-up when they reached the fire exit door, but as they had done regular fire drills in the past, nobody panicked, and the evacuation proceeded smoothly. Which is when a second explosion reverberated through the building, and when she looked behind her, she saw to her shock that the floor collapsed and that where she had been sitting before, working at her computer, a crater now gaped.

Looked like the entire building was about to collapse where they stood.

The next moment, panic did break out, and as people hustled and pushed and shoved to get out of there before the rest of the building crumbled into a mass of debris and twisted metal and broken glass, she just let herself be hustled along by the throng of bodies squeezing through the door. As she hurried down the metal fire escape, she saw that a woman had fallen and threatened to be trampled by the panicking thronging mass. So she quickly yanked the

EXCERPT FROM PURRFECT SPIDER (MAX 90)

woman back to her feet and assisted her in hurrying to safety.

The woman had lost her shoes, but that couldn't be helped. Better to lose one's shoes than one's life, after all. The moment they arrived at street level, they ran away from the building, putting as much distance between themselves and the disaster area as possible. She could already hear the sound of fire engines approaching. And that's when a third explosion rocked the building, this one even bigger than before. As they all watched in stupefaction, the entire structure came crashing down in a deafening roar, as if leveled by a giant monster. A gust of smoke and dust pummeled them and blew them off their feet. As she and her other colleagues struggled to get up, she saw that the office building where she had been so hard at work only half an hour before, was gone, replaced by dust and debris.

She hoped they had all made it out alive, and as she stared at the devastation, couldn't help but wonder if the man who had been staring at them from across the street had something to do with this. She searched the crowd, but there was no trace of him.

It could have been a coincidence, of course, but somehow she doubted it.

Which could only mean… that Ophelae had been the victim of an attack. A bombing. But then she shook off the silly notion. A gas explosion, that was probably what had happened. There was no other explanation. Or was there?

ABOUT NIC

Nic has a background in political science and before being struck by the writing bug worked odd jobs around the world (including but not limited to massage therapist in Mexico, gardener in Italy, restaurant manager in India, and Berlitz teacher in Belgium).

When he's not writing he enjoys curling up with a good (comic) book, watching British crime dramas, French comedies or Nancy Meyers movies, sampling pastry (apple cake!), pasta and chocolate (preferably the dark variety), twisting himself into a pretzel doing morning yoga, going for a brisk walk, and spoiling his feline assistants Lily and Ricky.

He lives with his wife (and aforementioned cats) in a small village smack dab in the middle of absolutely nowhere and is probably writing his next 'Mysteries of Max' book right now.

www.nicsaint.com

Printed in Great Britain
by Amazon